'What's the ma

Kyle's arms tightened around her as he continued, 'Is it this?' Lifting her face up to his, he kissed her lips fleetingly.

She nodded mutely and he did it again, and as her mouth sprang to life beneath his the years rolled away.

But maybe she was reading too much into it as, taking her key from her hand, he turned it in the lock and gently pushed her inside.

'Go to bed. I'll see you in the morning,' he said, and with a last backward look over his shoulder he went to find the lift.

I'll see you in the morning, he'd said, and it was true...he would...and the day after...and the day after that, she thought. Whatever he said or did, Kyle was back in her life again.

Abigail Gordon is fascinated by words, and what better way to use them than in the crafting of romance between the sexes—a state of the heart that has affected almost everyone at some time in their lives? Twice widowed, she now lives alone in a Cheshire village. Her two eldest sons between them have presented her with three delightful grandchildren, and her youngest son lives nearby.

Recent titles by the same author:

EMERGENCY REUNION

BY

ABIGAIL GORDON

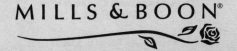

MILLS & BOON®

First published in Great Britain 2001
Harlequin Mills & Boon Limited,
Eton House, 18-24 Paradise Road, Richmond, Surrey TW9 1SR

© Abigail Gordon 2001

ISBN 0 263 82682 1

Set in Times Roman 10½ on 11½ pt.
03-0801-52843

Printed and bound in Spain
by Litografia Rosés, S.A., Barcelona

CHAPTER ONE

'WILL you, please, stand back and give the doctors some space and the injured person some privacy?' a police sergeant was brusquely asking of the crowd that had gathered at the scene of the accident.

Hannah flashed him a grateful glance. The fast-response team had been called out again into a busy London street. This time the victim was an elderly lady who'd been scuttling across the road in the middle of heavy traffic and had ended up trapped beneath a bus.

As the curious onlookers moved back reluctantly Hannah could feel it again, the strangeness of treating a patient in an outside situation instead of within the enclosed facilities of the accident and emergency units where she'd worked previously.

She was with Pete Stubbs this morning. It had been his turn to take her with him on a call-out during these first weeks of a six-month period with the helicopter medical service.

Her time spent with them would be the final part of her training before taking up a consultancy in accident and emergency at a hospital yet to be decided. They'd been called out the moment they'd reported for duty that morning, and once the helicopter had put in an appearance from the airfield where it was based at night, they'd left the helipad and operations room, amongst the rooftops of a London hospital, and had taken off into the morning sky.

'You're going to miss the arrival of the new chief,' one of the other doctors had called as Hannah and Pete Stubbs had sprinted towards the Eurocopter, collecting ready-packed medical kits and street maps on the way.

'Too bad,' the lanky doctor had called over his shoulder. 'We have a lady under a bus.'

Jack Krasner and his copilot had dropped them as near as possible to the scene of the accident, and as they'd crossed another busy road and skirted a small park, Hannah had checked the time. It had taken them three minutes to get airborne and another five to make the journey.

They'd brought a paramedic along, which was standard practice at the unit, and as the three of them came hurtling round the corner they saw that the fire brigade were in the process of jacking up the bus so that the victim could be pulled from underneath.

'I've got to check the lady out before we move her,' Pete said. 'There's no telling what state she might be in.'

'I'm going to crawl underneath,' he told the fire chief who was in charge of the lifting exercise. 'If there are spinal injuries she'll need a collar and almost certainly an injection to kill the pain before we start to move her.'

Hannah was observing the situation anxiously. This wasn't the first time she'd been out on an emergency and it was frustrating that for this first month she was only allowed to watch.

Once that period was over she would be the same as the others, left to make her own decisions on occasions such as this. But today Pete was in charge. Even so, it was like being thrown in at the deep end.

He had seen her expression and the tall, thin doctor, who'd been eyeing up the amount of space beneath the bus, said laconically, 'Fortunate that I'm just skin and bone, eh, Dr Morgan?'

He was less casual as he told her with brisk authority, 'Ring the trauma unit at the nearest hospital and warn them

The helicopter had been hovering over the rooftops in the light summer night like a plump-breasted, clattering bird as Hannah had come out of the theatre the night before the incident involving the bus. But unlike a bird its plumage was of bright metal, its wings whirring propellers.

She'd felt her nerve endings tighten. The fast-response team had been called out again into the busy London streets, and she'd wondered who it had been this time who'd needed them so desperately that the saving of a life might depend on the speed with which they touched down.

A month ago she would have witnessed the helicopter's progress through the night sky and thought little of it, but since then she'd become one of them…part of the unit that was always at the ready, waiting in the operations room beside the helipad on the roof of a nearby hospital.

They were doctors who took to the sky within minutes of call-out. To the critically injured or very sick the sight of their brightly coloured surgical suits was a sign that help was indeed at hand.

She'd done a year in general practice, then had worked as a registrar in Accident and Emergency at a hospital in northern England for some years and now, had decided to spend six months working with the helicopter medics, and one couldn't get any closer to the nitty-gritty of Accident and Emergency than that.

It was the longest that doctors in training stayed with them because of the excessive trauma the job brought with it, and most of them, on completing the allowed time, went on to specialise as accident and emergency consultants in various hospitals around the country.

Hannah had been there just two weeks and it was her day off, hence the visit to the theatre. But it was long enough for her to feel that she belonged as the helicopter whirred on its way above the chimneypots on a golden evening.

She felt Richard's eyes on her, and even before she'd

turned to face him she was bracing herself against the chill that anything connected with her new job brought forth.

He was always irritated with her these days. She hadn't been sure that she would be able to go to the play until the last minute because of the duty rotas, and that had annoyed him.

When he'd seen her in the dazzling surgical suit which had taken the place of her dignified doctor's white coat he'd been even more disparaging.

'You don't expect me to jump out of the chopper in the middle of the carnage of an accident in a London street in a white coat, do you?' she'd said protestingly when he'd commented on the size and brightness of the outfit. 'We need to be seen when we're out there amongst the traffic, or we could end up as casualties ourselves.'

She'd had to admit that it wasn't the most charismatic clothing she'd ever worn, but its roomy proportions allowed movement in restricted situations and that was what it was all about.

She was small and slender, with silver blonde hair cut in a short bob and wide blue eyes that were the clear pools of an uncomplicated mind. Hannah Morgan was twenty-nine years old and unattached, and there was no likelihood of her tetchy theatre companion filling the breach.

They'd known each other when she'd worked in Manchester, and had travelled on the same train each morning. Richard Jarvis had been employed in a stockbroker's office and Hannah had been working in Accident and Emergency at a nearby hospital.

He'd been likeable enough then. But moving to a better job in London and up the social scale had made him not quite so pleasant and, though he didn't know it, this was to be their last meeting.

The young doctor had looked him up because she hadn't known anyone else in London and she was lonely. But

Hannah had decided that being alone was preferable to being alternately criticised and patronised by the likes of Richard.

She didn't know what ailed him and didn't particularly care. It wasn't as if she was looking for a relationship and maybe that was what was getting to him.

On that score he wouldn't be the first. She was attractive to the opposite sex and was always ready to socialise, but that was all. Hannah had only ever been really in love once, and to say that it had been a disaster would have been the understatement of all time. So much so that she'd never been ready to test the water since.

'So, when are we going to get together again?' Richard said as they waited for a taxi.

'We're not,' she told him calmly, 'and if you want to know why, Richard, just take a good look at yourself. You have no claim on me and I'm not prepared to continue listening to your critical comments about everything that concerns me.

'If my job doesn't have the appeal of the wards and the white coat, too bad. You might be glad to see someone from my team one day. None of us knows what lies around the next corner.'

And on that parting shot she got into the taxi that had just pulled up and left him standing on the pavement.

'Good to have you with us, Hannah,' a burly, middle-aged man had said when she'd presented herself at the unit on her first day with the team. 'We've got a guy on leave at the moment so your presence is very welcome. And we're expecting a new chief.

'The A and E consultant you saw when you came for interview has had to take early retirement due to family problems and we have a new guy starting in a couple of weeks' time.'

He'd gone on to say, 'I'm Graham Smith, consultant anaesthetist, known as Smitty to the guys here at the operations centre.' He'd pointed to a lanky six-footer engrossed in the morning paper. 'This is Dr Pete Stubbs.'

'Hi, there,' the man in question said with a grin.

As she smiled back at him she said, 'I can't see me being much use until I know the ropes. For one thing I've never been in a helicopter.'

They both nodded understandingly and the other man told her, 'You'll just be observing for the first month so don't fret about not knowing the routine. After a couple of trips in the helicopter you'll be as easy with it as we are. It's what's waiting for you when you disembark that takes getting used to. We doctors are inclined to take the ambulance services for granted, but in this job we're right in there with them...on the ground.

'Have you met the operations officer?' he asked, and when she shook her head he said, 'Come on. I'll introduce you. As the calls come in to the ambulance service centre at Waterloo they're monitored by a specially trained paramedic, and if that person thinks that there's major trauma involved they put a call through to our operations officer here and we swing into action.

'We've only the one helicopter, so if there's more than one call-out required our man here has to decide where the need is greatest. In those circumstances any other situations have to be served by ambulance.'

As they walked together along the rooftop helipad he explained, 'The chief would normally show you round but, as I've explained, we're in the middle of a change-over and this new guy is an unknown quantity to all of us. Apparently he's been doing the same job abroad and is very highly thought of in many quarters. He should have received the paperwork regarding your appointment to the unit and, no doubt, he'll agree with the rest of us that you're going to brighten up the place,' he said with a mischievous twinkle in his eye.

She managed a weak smile at the compliment and said doubtfully, 'I see.'

So to the senior medic on the outfit she would be an unknown quantity when he arrived. Meeting him would be a pleasure still to come. But she comforted herself with the thought that they would all be strangers to him.

The first time she'd gone on a call-out it had been an incident where a teenage boy had collapsed with a heart attack during rugby practice at a local school and the helicopter pilots had taken them right down onto the playing fields.

It had been touch and go for the boy but the quick arrival of the two doctors, and the immediate resuscitation they'd given him, had prevented what might have been a fatal cardiac arrest.

And making the end result even more satisfying had been the quick flight over the rooftops to a nearby hospital for further treatment.

Altogether, the work was very rewarding. There was none of the frustration often felt in a hospital situation, where delays of all kinds frayed the nerves. She was involved in a branch of health care that covered extreme emergencies, and as such there were two ways to describe it—satisfying, and exhausting.

Tomorrow they would be a full team again, she'd thought as she'd paid off the taxi after leaving Richard to make his own way home. The doctor who'd been on leave would be back and the new chief would be at the helm.

There'd been the odd reference to him during the two weeks she'd been part of the unit, and she'd noticed that if enthusiasm had been lacking when he'd been mentioned, there had been no shortage of respect.

So what was it going to be? Hannah had wondered as she'd wedged herself onto the tube at just gone seven o'clock the next morning. The prescription as before? Or a new broom sweeping clean?

As the latest addition to the team, it shouldn't make much difference either way as far as she was concerned. But what of the others—Graham Smith, Pete Stubbs, the operations officer, paramedics and Dr David Wainright who was due back from leave today? How were they going to cope with the new chief?

There was no immediate answer to that question as when she arrived at the operations room they were all drinking mugs of tea, with the new chief nowhere in sight. As Hannah had poured herself a cup the clock had eased itself on to half past seven and another working day began. Soon the helicopter would arrive from the airfield where it had spent the night and by eight o'clock they would be fully functional.

On this particular morning the first call had come through just as the chopper was touching down on the roof and by five past eight Pete and herself were airborne to attend the accident in a London street.

The last thing she'd been expecting was having to cope with the emergency on her own, but Pete's injury beneath the bus altered everything.

And then what had happened? she asked herself as they flew back to base after depositing the old lady with the trauma team.

She'd looked up from her position on the ground to find Kyle looking down on her. Older, with the same dark thatch of hair, his shoulders broader than those of the young registrar of the mercurial mind and short fuse of long ago. But still with the same lean attractiveness.

Jack Krasner, the amiable pilot, had observed her pale face and he said, 'Shook you up, that business under the bus, didn't it, Doc? Or was it finding the new chief standing over you that did it?'

Hannah had dredged up a smile. 'It was a bit of both, I think, Jack.'

The rest of the team were waiting for her, their eyes anxious.

'What's this about Pete?' Graham Smith asked. 'The new chief has arrived and he tells us he was there, at the scene.'

'Pete was crawling under the bus when it moved,' she told them. 'He lost consciousness from a knock on the head. They've taken him to Charing Cross, but he seemed to be all right apart from the gash on his head.'

She was aware of the office door being closed and could see the dark shadow of its occupant through the glass. What had he been doing at the scene of the accident? she wondered. If she was going to be confronted with that particular face from the past, it would have been kinder for it to have been now, rather than on her stomach in the grime of a busy street.

He must have heard her voice. 'Will you come in, please, Dr Morgan?' he called and aware that she was a mass of frayed nerves, she obeyed.

Pointing to the chair opposite the desk, Kyle said, 'Take a seat.' And as her eyes raked his face with the same intensity that a starving man might have observed food, Hannah saw that there were creases around the eyes which had once melted at the sight of her and tiny threads of silver in his hair.

'So you're not in America any more?' she said jerkily in an attempt to break the ice.

That remark brought forth a facial contortion that was something between a smile and a grimace. 'Does it look like it?'

'No, of course not. That was a stupid thing to say.'

He shrugged as if it was of no matter. 'I never went to America. I got a better offer to work in Queensland.'

'Australia!' she croaked. 'So that's why…'

Her voice trailed away. She wasn't going to tell him how hard she'd searched for him, not after all this time, and his next words showed it to have been a wise decision.

'This is the last place I would have ever thought to come across you,' he said tonelessly. 'I'd have expected you and that brother-in-law of yours to have nested long ago, but I see that it's still Hannah Morgan.'

The first shock was passing and pain was taking its place. So she hadn't been forgiven. Kyle hadn't believed her then and she was damned if she was going to go through the motions of protesting her innocence now. They'd broken up years ago and yet the sight of him still made her weak with longing.

'Yes, I'm still Hannah Morgan,' she said coolly, 'and Paul has made a new nest…but not with me.' Before he could comment on that piece of information she went on, 'Is there something you want to discuss with me?'

His eyes flicked over her face and Hannah saw a pulse quicken in his neck, but his voice was cool enough as he replied, 'Yes. I see from the information I have before me that you are specialising in accident and emergency, and that your six months with the helicopter unit will be the final part of your training.'

She nodded without speaking and he went on, 'Strange that we should both be in the same branch of health care.'

'And stranger still that we should find ourselves in the same unit,' she commented tightly. 'How long have you been back in England?'

'Two days this time. I came over a few weeks ago to inspect the set-up here and then went back to tie up all the loose ends in Australia.'

What loose ends were those? she wondered. Selling a house? Persuading a wife and family that life in the UK would be just fine?

It was eight years since they'd parted. The Kyle Templeton she'd known then had been fiery and ambitious, but passionate, too. He would have found someone to cuddle up to on cold winter nights somewhere along the way, which was more than she had.

'I'm told that new recruits to the team spend the first month merely observing,' he was saying, as if the brief mention of his affairs was sufficient.

He must have known that she would be interested, but he wasn't going to satisfy her curiosity and she wasn't going to ask. Kyle had invited her into his office to discuss the job. No doubt the fact that she was a blast from the past was now immaterial.

'Yes, that's right,' she agreed, as if talking to the only man she'd ever loved, after what seemed like a barren lifetime, meant nothing. 'I've done two weeks already and will feel less of an ornament when the month is up.'

'Hmm. I can imagine,' he murmured, with his eyes on the paperwork on the desk. 'How do you feel about it…being part of one of the fastest emergency services in the country?'

Hannah smiled. They were on an even footing now, and though her heart was still racing she was in control. It would be tonight when she got back to her silent flat that the impact of this incredible meeting would hit her the most.

'I love it. The lack of delay in getting to the patient. The challenge to the doctors as they spill out of the helicopter and charge to the scene of a major trauma. The friendliness here in the operations room…'

She didn't know whether it was nerves that were making

her so voluble or a desire to labour the point that, though he might be in charge, she'd got settled in before him.

Whatever it was, with every second that passed Hannah was becoming more aware that for the next few months she was going to be in close contact with the man who had once been in love with her and had then turned his back on her in cold anger.

'Mmm. Quite so,' he said blandly, as if she weren't the only one who was aware that she was gabbling. He lifted his head at that point and his next words were of dismissal. 'That will be all for now. Carry on observing with the different members of the team until I tell you otherwise.' And as if to emphasise that he had done with her, Kyle Templeton picked up the phone and began to dial.

'So what do you think of the new chief?' Graham Smith asked when she went back to join the others.

'Impressive,' she told him weakly.

It was true. He'd had style when she'd known him before, but the man with whom she'd just had that strange conversation in the office made the impetuous young medical registrar of long ago pale into insignificance.

The fire seemed to have gone, leaving a sort of cold gravity, but, then, she supposed that he was hardly likely to receive her with open arms after the way they'd parted.

But none of that mattered. If he'd made her heart beat faster before, now it was thundering in her ears. What a pity that Kyle hadn't been similarly affected.

Nothing had changed, she thought raggedly. Absence hadn't made the heart grow fonder as far as he was concerned, but she'd already decided that he wouldn't still be unattached, and the sight of a two-timing girlfriend from way back wasn't going to rock his foundations.

A call had just come through from the ambulance emergency centre reporting a man with serious head injuries after a fall from the window of a fourth-floor flat, and

Hannah's reflections had to be put on hold as she accompanied Smitty and one of the paramedics to the scene of the accident.

He was taking charge of the main call-out team for that day after Pete's accident and had full use of the helicopter. Any other emergencies would be dealt with by the others, using an ambulance.

Hannah had soon discovered that when a call for the helicopter service came through, everybody ran, doctors, paramedics and the two pilots grabbing ordnance survey maps, monitors and medical kits as they whizzed past.

In this case the victim's obvious injuries were severe, and while the paramedic was cutting off his clothes to make sure they weren't missing any other damage, Smitty was preparing to give him an injection that would put him to sleep. But first he tried to coax the patient into giving his name and address as a sign that his thought processes were still working.

The reply was a slurred jumble of words and, pointing to a huge swelling on the side of the man's head, Smitty said, 'We need to get this guy to the nearest hospital for a CT scan as fast as we can. There's a haematoma there if I'm not mistaken. But first I'm going to have to insert a breathing tube as he's no longer able to breathe on his own.'

'We'll take him to the Royal London Hospital,' he said when that had been accomplished. 'It's not exactly the nearest but they're more geared up to head injuries than some of the others in the area.'

While the inert figure was being carefully placed into the helicopter he rang to alert the trauma team at the hospital, and Hannah thought thankfully that yet another serious injury would be receiving the fast treatment only they could provide.

'Suspected haematoma on the left-hand side of the head,'

he told them with brief clarity. 'Deep lacerations to the skull and neck area and possible fracture of the ribcage, forearms and pelvis.'

When they got back to base the office door was open this time and Hannah heard Kyle Templeton say, 'I know that it isn't a cheap service that we're running here and that the health authorities' funding of over a million a year is a heck of a lot of money. I've just come from Australia. In fact, this is my first day with the helicopter service over here, and I have to tell you that it was no different there. Always threatening cuts to one of the most efficient accident and emergency teams ever created.'

As Hannah made to move on, his broad back was towards her, but almost as if he sensed her presence Kyle swivelled round in his chair and beckoned her to enter.

He was actually smiling as he told the person on the other end of the phone, 'No need to apologise. You weren't to know that you were talking to the new boy. But uninitiated though I may be, I can tell you without even checking that we need every cent of funding we can get.'

A step behind her in the open doorway heralded the arrival of Jack Krasner, the pilot, who had already asked her for a date.

He was a pleasant change from the nit-picking Richard, but up to the moment Hannah had met Kyle Templeton again she'd been more interested in the job than new friendships with the opposite sex.

The man behind the desk had put the phone down and was eyeing the pilot questioningly. 'You said that you wanted to go over the chopper with me, sir,' Jack said.

'Yes, Jack,' Kyle said briskly. 'Give me a couple of minutes and I'll be with you.'

'Did you want me for something?' Hannah asked when the other man had gone.

'Er...yes, and don't think I intend to make a habit of

having private conversations with you. The last thing I have in mind is for you to be closeted in here with me all the time.'

'I can quite easily believe that,' she told him with a bland sort of pleasantness that hid the hurt the remark had brought forth.

Dark eyes were studying her thoughtfully and she thought that if Kyle had something to say, why didn't he get on with it?

He was about to do so.

'There are a couple of things I want to say to you,' he said levelly. 'First of all, I've had time to adjust to our unexpected meeting and I see no reason why past happenings should intrude upon our work here. We are both adults and it was all a long time ago.'

'Absolutely,' she agreed calmly, as her spirits plummeted.

What was he expecting her to do? Claim a previous acquaintance with him in front of the others? Surely Kyle didn't still feel bitter about their break-up?

Yet maybe he did. Strong, passionate, loyal, his hadn't been a forgiving nature and it looked as if nothing had changed with regard to that.

'And secondly,' he was continuing, 'I need temporary accommodation…smartish. I'm in a hotel at the moment amongst a clutter of luggage and other personal belongings and it's not good.'

Hannah's eyes widened. 'I take it that you're not asking if I've got a spare room…if your previous comment is anything to go by. That it's more a case of do I know of a vacant house or flat?'

He nodded and she had to admire the cheek of him. One moment he was well and truly putting her in her place and the next was asking her to help him house-hunt.

'So you're on your own, then?' she questioned as the image of the wife and family receded. No wife or children?'

'I've brought no baggage with me, if that's what you're asking,' he answered, and, as if he really was out to rile her, added, 'He travels fastest who travels alone, don't you think?

'What about you?' he went on as she glared at him. 'The name's the same but that doesn't mean that you're not tucked up in a cosy little love nest.'

'I think that's my business, don't you?'

She wasn't going to tell him that no man had ever equalled him in looks, character and charisma, although that last characteristic seemed to be in short supply so far.

For the first time his cool composure faltered. 'Yes, of course it is. I shouldn't have asked,' he said in a low voice.

'There's a penthouse apartment in the same block as mine,' she said perversely, having handed out the rebuff. 'It's way above the rest of them in position and price, but would probably suit a high flyer such as you.'

His head came up at that. 'If that was sarcasm it's wasted on me, I'm afraid.' He pulled a sheet of paper towards him. 'Where is it?'

As Hannah gave him the address and telephone number of the letting agents, he looked up enquiringly. 'How far from the helipad is it?'

'A couple of miles. I come in by tube. But, you know, there will be other vacant flats in the city...if you've got time to chase them up.'

The thought of having Kyle living in the same complex made her heart leap, but there was no way that she was going to appear too eager.

He nodded. 'No doubt. But time is what I haven't got. Anyway, thanks for the information, and now I must seek out Jack Krasner, who's going to give me the lowdown on our specially adapted Eurocopter.'

But Kyle didn't move immediately when she'd left to join the others. He remained seated at the desk, his face sombre in the light from the window.

He was being a miserable blighter with Hannah. He admitted it, but finding her as part of the helicopter response team earlier in the day had stunned him.

When he'd seen her name on the paperwork his predecessor had left for him he'd been sure it would be another woman of the same name. To discover that it wasn't and that she was just as beautiful as he remembered had thrown him into such a state of disbelief that he'd felt the hard approach was the only way not to make a fool of himself.

And now, after warning her off, he'd asked Hannah of all people if she could help him find somewhere to live. He must be crackers!

It wouldn't be surprising if he was. Today of all days he'd wanted to be on top form as he took over the reins on the helipad. He'd been highly recommended for the job and was keen to show those who'd appointed him that they'd made a wise decision, and what had happened?

He'd seen the Eurocopter in the sky above as he'd driven to the unit where he was going to be based and had followed it, wanting to see at first hand how his staff would handle the situation that awaited them.

But he'd had a surprise and they didn't come any bigger. The past had leapt out at him in the form of a slender blonde doctor, and everything else had become of secondary importance.

'Get a grip on yourself, Templeton,' he told himself. 'She didn't answer when you asked if she was in a relationship, and even if she isn't, there's nothing colder than love that's gone off the boil.'

All very profound reasoning, but it didn't stop him from ringing the house agents before he went to find Jack, and that turned out to be an abortive errand as while he'd been discussing the vacant apartment a call had come through from the ambulance emergency services and the Eurocopter was ready for take off.

As Graham Smith, Hannah and a paramedic hurriedly climbed on board, the operations officer called across, 'An iron gate has fallen onto a child at a primary school in Battersea, sir. There are serious injuries from the sound of it.'

'Then what are they waiting for?' he asked abruptly, as a vision of Ben in a similar situation made him break into a sweat.

But as he well knew, the helicopter emergency service wasn't waiting for anything. It never did. That was the whole point of its existence, and as the raucous clatter of the helicopter drowned all other sounds it rose into the early evening sky and one of the strangest days of both their lives drew a little nearer to its close.

CHAPTER TWO

A SUMMER sun was setting over London as Hannah stood on the pavement below the helipad, waiting to hail the first empty taxi that came along.

The tube was all right in the morning, but not at this hour when the crowds had gone and the platforms were less busy. She'd tried it once and had been unnerved at the sight of loiterers on the stairways and passages.

Smitty and the others had gone to the pub for a quick drink before making their way home and she'd been invited to go with them, but the need to be by herself was overwhelming.

Her mind was in chaos. Had been from the moment she'd seen Kyle. And though she was proud of the way she'd handled herself, now that she was out of the building and away from him she could feel herself crumbling.

The day had seemed never-ending for more reasons than one. Not only had his presence on the unit made her aware of every minute, but at this time of year days were long and the helicopter emergency service was on call from half past seven in the morning until sunset.

Any emergencies once daylight had gone were dealt with by ambulance, the authorities being of the opinion that it would be dangerous for the helicopter to be flying around the city during the hours of darkness.

As a black cab came whizzing round the corner she stepped forward to hail it—only to discover that the day wasn't yet over as far as she and Kyle were concerned.

'I'll join you if I may,' his voice said from behind. 'I believe that we're both going in the same direction. My hotel isn't far from your apartment block.' As she turned round slowly he added, 'That is, if you're going home?'

'Of course I'm going home,' she said edgily, dismayed that she was back to watching what she said and did. 'Where else would I be going at this time of night after being on the go since seven this morning?'

'I've no idea,' he said calmly, and as the taxi driver cleared his throat to remind them that he was still there, Kyle took her arm and opened the door.

'So how has your first day gone?' she asked politely as the vehicle moved off.

It was a crazy question to ask. He might just tell her that it had been going all right until she'd appeared on the scene.

'Fine. I've a lot of experience in the accident and emergency services and this unit is the type that I prefer the most. Obviously every set-up is different but I soon adjust.'

Hannah relaxed. If he was going to talk shop that was fine. She could cope with that. Making sure that he continued to do so, she said, 'Will you be office-based, or can we expect you to go out on call?'

'Both. I shall certainly be going out with the teams. You might recall that I'm more of an action man than a pen-pusher...if you can take your mind back that far.'

The trap was there and she fell into it. 'Yes, I do recall that. I also remember that some of your actions were extremely hasty.'

That brought his head round to face her in the shadowed taxi. 'That's a matter of opinion, wouldn't you say?'

'No. I wouldn't. It's the truth,' she told him steadily.

The taxi driver called over his shoulder, 'Is this where you want dropping off, madam?'

Hannah said, 'Yes, thanks.' And before Kyle could reply, she was gone.

Once inside the flat she threw herself into the nearest

chair. She'd just done the very thing she'd vowed not to. Tried to justify herself to a man who probably hadn't given her a thought in years. Where was her pride?

The phone was ringing when Kyle went into his hotel room and when he picked it up his mother's voice came over the line.

'Hi, Mum,' he said with a lift to his voice. 'How's Ben?'

'Fast asleep,' she said. 'He wanted to wait up for you, but we kept trying to get you and there was no answer. So in the end I said that I'd ask you to ring him first thing in the morning.'

'He's not fretting, is he?' he asked anxiously. He was aware that moving to a new country was a big enough step for a seven-year-old, without being placed with grandparents he only saw rarely.

'He's missing you, of course,' his mother replied, 'but apart from that he's enjoying the village school, and loves playing with all the toys your dad has bought him. Those two are getting on like a house on fire.'

'That's great,' Kyle enthused. 'Once I've got settled into the job I'll look for a house with a garden and advertise for a good housekeeper. In the meantime I'm about to rent an apartment which will do for the time being until I've sorted out a proper home for him.'

'There's no rush as far as we're concerned,' his mother said. 'We love having him.'

'I know you do, Mum,' he said gently, 'and I suppose you think that a Cotswold village would be a better place for him than amid the London smog, but I'm missing him already and it is where my job is.'

'Yes, dear, I know that. We do understand, you know.'

When she'd gone off the line he stood staring into space. He doubted if anyone, even his mother, understood how much Ben meant to him. Maybe it was because he'd been left to bring him up on his own.

He'd been in a strange mood during those first months in Queensland all that time ago. Bitter and resentful at the way he'd been let down by Hannah, he'd let a nurse at the hospital where he'd been working make a play for him, and in no time at all she'd been telling him she was pregnant.

The news had brought him up with a jolt, and when she'd announced that she was going to give the baby up for adoption he'd been filled with self loathing. Wanting to make things right, Kyle had managed to persuade the mother to give him sole custody of the child. Marriage had never been discussed. Both sides had been glad to be free of each other, and by the time the baby was born she had already moved on to another man. Kyle had become a single parent and he'd been determined that Ben would have all the love and security he could ever want.

He'd told Hannah that he was alone in London and at that moment it was true, but not for long. He'd seen no reason to start explaining that he was responsible for a child he had fathered within months of their break-up.

For one thing he wouldn't come out of it as having been exactly devastated at the end of their affair. The fact that he'd let bitterness overcome common sense was a weak excuse and, anyway, Kyle wasn't the sort of man who made excuses.

Back in Australia it had been easy enough to arrange his domestic life, with an excellent nanny during Ben's first years and then, when he'd started school, a motherly house-keeper.

He'd intended that it should be the same here once he'd got his bearings, but meeting up with Hannah again had thrown him completely.

He was missing Ben, missing him a lot, but today's happenings had taken his mind off it for a while. Hannah was back in his life. On the edge of it maybe, but back in his sphere nevertheless, and amongst the tortuous thoughts that had been going round in his mind was the realisation that if things had worked out differently he and she might have had children of their own by now.

But that clinging-vine brother-in-law of hers had put paid to that, and she'd been willing to let him do so if what he'd seen on the ghastly morning when he'd walked in on them had been anything to go by.

So why had nothing come of it? Hannah had said that Paul had married again, but it hadn't been to her. What a mess it had all been. And now she was telling him that he'd been too quick to jump to conclusions. But she would, wouldn't she? She'd said it often enough at the time, but he'd been too enraged to listen.

However, he'd changed a lot since then. He was more patient, not as idealistic and fiery, and, that being so, could he endure six months of them working side by side?

Hannah awoke feeling hot and sticky in a humid dawn. She'd made herself a hot chocolate and then gone straight to bed when she'd got in. She'd decided that the only way she would get to sleep was by not letting herself look back over the day's events, and it had worked.

But she hadn't allowed for her subconscious and she'd dreamt of Kyle for most of the night. He'd been forgiving, welcoming her with open arms, but as she'd been about to throw herself into them he'd changed into Paul, her brother-in-law, and she'd pushed him away.

Her mouth was dry, her head ached, and going to the French windows of her bedroom she stepped out onto a small balcony that overlooked a park down below.

It was only half past four and yet it was daylight. Outside, the deafening throb of London was tuned down to a hum that would soon be back to its full volume, and in just two and a half hours she would be on her way back to the operations room beside the helipad...and Kyle would be there.

And if he took the penthouse at the top of the apartment building, she wouldn't just be in his orbit on the job, he would be encroaching into her private life, too.

So what's wrong with that? a voice inside her said. Why don't you make the most of it, instead of being so defeatist? The fates once did you a very bad turn. Maybe they're out to make amends.

All the major traumas that the helicopter service dealt with were followed up, mainly to prove its importance to those funding the unit.

Not all of those they were called out to recovered. Sometimes the condition of the patient was so critical that no power on earth could have saved them. Others had died before they'd even got to them. But many of those attended by the team had lived, due to prompt attention on the spot and the fast transfer to hospital.

There was news on the small girl who'd been crushed by the school gate the previous day, and it wasn't good. They'd arrived at the scene to find that she'd had head, chest and possible pelvic injuries, and at one time her heart had stopped beating.

Grim-faced, Smitty and the paramedic had worked on her and when they'd got her heart restarted the frantic dash to the nearest hospital had begun. The trauma team had been waiting on the rooftop for her arrival, and after they'd been put in the picture she had been rushed into Theatre.

As Hannah and the two men had been leaving, her parents had arrived, the father white-faced and the mother hysterical.

'Heads will roll for this one,' Smitty had said sombrely.

'There should be better maintenance to school property than that.'

And now the follow-up report had come in. The child was in Intensive Care. Hopefully there would be no brain damage due to the prompt restarting of the heart, but her injuries were severe.

Hannah was the last to arrive on the unit. She'd overslept, having gone back to bed for a couple of hours after her disturbed night, and only caught the tail end of the message.

Graham had filled her in and then amazed her by saying, 'Kyle Templeton was saying that he can imagine how the girl's parents are feeling as, like some of us, he's got a child of his own. Apparently the kid's staying with his parents somewhere in the Cotswolds until he finds a suitable house here in London. There was no mention of a wife, though.'

Hannah was goggling at him. Kyle had a child! He'd never said. But, then, why should he? The man didn't have to unburden himself to her of all people. But, as Graham had just said, where was his wife?

Her newly made resolution to make the best of what the fates were offering died at birth as jealousy swept over her.

She didn't want Kyle to have given his heart to another woman. Childish and ridiculous though it might be, she just didn't. Which meant that she'd been expecting him to have lived like a monk all those years. Some hope!

Yet she hadn't exactly lived a life of celibacy either. But there'd never been anyone to take his place. If she could have found him during that time she would have insisted until he'd believed her that any passion he'd witnessed between herself and her brother-in-law had all been on Paul's side.

She would have made him understand what she'd suffered for looking like her dead twin sister and how, because she'd sympathised with Paul's grief, she hadn't fought him off quickly enough when he wouldn't release her from that disastrous kiss.

Kyle was talking to the operations officer, unaware that Hannah and Graham were discussing him, but when he looked up the other man had gone and just Hannah was there, eyeing him questioningly.

'What is it?' he asked as he came across. 'You're looking very serious.'

She dredged up a smile. 'Am I? Perhaps it's because I've just learned that you have a son.'

'Oh, that. I see. What difference does it make?'

Do rub it in, she thought grimly. If my life has been on hold, it would appear that yours hasn't.

'You said that you hadn't brought anyone with you,' she pointed out with chilly exactness.

'I said that I had no one with me here in London, which was true. Ben is with my parents in Gloucestershire for the time being, but I'm sure that you aren't interested in my domestic affairs.'

'You're right. I'm not.'

'Fair enough, but I might be interested in yours,' he said, unperturbed. 'Let's have a bite together at lunchtime and you can tell me how life has been treating you in recent years.'

'I doubt you'll find what I have to say very interesting,' she said coolly, wondering just what he was leading up to. 'Perhaps you're feeling that as you've been landed with me for the next few months you might as well try to get to know me…again.'

Cool, dark eyes locked with hers. 'Perhaps I am,' he said with the same calm smoothness. 'One o'clock, shall we say?'

'All right,' Hannah agreed, unable to pass by the chance of talking to him about something other than the job. 'But won't it be going against what you said yesterday...no cosy chats?'

'Did I say that?' Kyle said blandly.

'Yes, you did,' she countered, 'and the fact that we are already known to each other won't be under wraps for long if we're seen lunching together on what is only your second day on the unit.'

'How do you know that it won't be seen as my having met you and liked what I saw, that I'm moving in on you before anybody else does?'

'If that should be the case I would have to inform them that it was about as likely as pigs being able to fly.'

He ignored that. 'One o'clock it is, then.' And he went back to continue his discussion with the operations officer.

They didn't lunch together. At one o'clock Hannah was at the side of the M25, watching a desperately injured man being treated by David Wainright and one of the paramedics.

The police had stopped the traffic and an ambulance had been already there when the helicopter had touched down on the motorway and they were greeted with the news that the patient had thrown himself off an overhead bridge into the path of the traffic below.

'It's incredible that there wasn't a pile-up,' a grim-faced police sergeant said. 'If he'd landed in front of, or on top of, an oncoming car it would have been chaos, but by a miracle he didn't and the only person the poor devil hurt is himself.'

The man was semi-conscious, unable to move his legs and far too badly injured to speak, but every time they touched him he groaned.

'We're going to have to ease him onto a spinal board before we put him in the chopper,' David said, adding with a quick glance at Hannah who was standing anxiously beside him, 'You're going to have to give a hand, Dr Morgan.'

'While I'm getting him onto the board, phone the hospital with details of his injuries. Tell them that at first examination they appear to be many and serious, especially the lack of movement in the legs.'

Even as he was telling her what to say, David was getting ready to lift the patient off the ground with the help of the paramedic and two of the ambulance men. Each man took part of the blanket he was lying on to make a hammock shape that would prevent jarring.

When that had been accomplished David eyed her questioningly. 'Are they going to be ready for us?'

'Yes,' she said briskly, eager to be involved.

Once they were finally airborne, Hannah reflected on her position in the team. It gave her no pleasure, having to watch when she wanted to be part of the action. Admittedly she'd had no experience of these sorts of conditions. Her role previously had been more like that of one of the trauma team that would be waiting on the hospital roof for the arrival of this attempted suicide victim.

But she was raring to go and in ten days' time she would be allowed to participate in whatever emergency surgery was required when there was a call out.

She was the only woman presently on the team and she intended to let the others see that she knew her stuff... especially Kyle Templeton.

The thought of him reminded her that they'd been intending to have lunch together, but the desperate action of a despairing man had put paid to that and she didn't know whether to be relieved or sorry.

Once they'd reached the hospital and the trauma team had taken over, they didn't leave immediately. The two doctors stayed in the corridor outside the resuscitation unit and waited for news on the man's condition. They'd already been told he would be lucky to pull through and it wasn't hard to believe, considering the extent of his injuries.

This was where it was different from being in the usual accident and emergency set-up, Hannah thought. In the places where she'd worked before they'd taken over from the local ambulance crews and gone on from there, treating the patients in Casualty with a triage nurse there to decide who should be seen first, according to the seriousness of their condition.

But there was no need for picking and choosing in the helicopter emergency service because every patient they brought in was in a life-threatening state. The fact that their part in the scheme of things was over once they'd delivered the sufferer into the best possible care sometimes created a feeling of anticlimax, and both Hannah and David Wainright were loth to leave for that reason.

A doctor came out and David went to speak to him. As they talked Hannah rang Kyle to give him an update.

'Where are you?' he asked briskly.

'We're at King's Hospital. Hanging on until we know just how serious the patient's condition is. The pilots have gone for a quick coffee and David is talking to one of the trauma team. Do you want to speak to him?'

'No, not yet. I want a word with you first. Are you coping?'

'Er…yes.'

'You don't sound very sure.'

'It's just that I can understand why the likes of myself are only allowed to work on the unit for a short time. The stress is so much more than in the kind of accident and emergency situations I've been in before.'

'Well, of course it is,' he agreed. 'On this unit we're in the thick of it. I agree that it's the most stressful health-care situation that any of us have ever worked in, but we never find anyone asking to be allowed to opt out.'

'Naturally,' she agreed coolly.

Was he administering a rebuke? Did Kyle think she wasn't up to it because she'd dared to express some concern?

He didn't need to. She would show him! He might have no time for her in any other area of his life, but when it came to the job he wasn't going to be able to fault her.

'Tell David not to be too long there. Another call could come through at any time,' he was saying as if the subject was closed, and on that he hung up. When she turned round David was beside her, his face less sombre than before.

'The guy is hanging in there,' he said. 'Was that Kyle?'

Hannah nodded, thankful that the conversation was over.

It was the middle of the afternoon when they got back and she was starving. A piece of toast before she'd left home was the only food she'd had and the pull of hunger found her heading for the restaurant on the floor below.

With a pot of tea and a sandwich in front of her she began to unwind, but not for long. When she looked up Kyle was making his way towards her and her heart began to beat faster as it always did when he was around.

'I imagine that you're ready for that,' he said calmly as he looked down on her. 'Do you mind if I join you for a moment?'

'No, of course not,' she said quietly. 'What can I do for you?'

She'd taken off the claustrophobic surgical suit, and dark eyes were taking in her silver fairness and the sleeveless white top and lightweight black trousers she was wearing underneath for coolness.

Hannah could feel her cheeks warming. What was he thinking? she wondered. That a petite blonde such as herself stuck out like a sore finger amongst these fast-thinking, fast-moving, male medics?

Or was his mind winging back to that other time when they'd been madly in love? Maybe she ought to make the first move, in spite of telling him she wasn't interested in his affairs.

'You say that your son is with your parents. Is your wife there, too?' she asked casually. Her mouth had gone dry and her heart was hammering against her ribs as she waited for an answer.

'I haven't got a wife.'

'Why? Are you divorced?'

'No.'

'So…?'

'I had an affair.'

She swallowed hard. So he *had* found somebody to snuggle up to on cold nights. Suddenly she didn't want to know any more. Every moment of that wretched time was etched on her mind for ever and yet here was Kyle calmly telling her he'd had an affair and had fathered a child from it.

She sensed that he was waiting for her to ask who it had been with and how he came to have the boy, but she wasn't going to oblige.

'Yes. I see,' she said dismissively.

His smile was taut. 'I wonder if you do. But what about you, Hannah? You were so close to that brother-in-law of yours I would have expected you to have filled the gap your sister left. That was what he had in mind all along, wasn't it?'

Don't start protesting your innocence, the voice of pride was saying. The damage was done long ago. Let Kyle think what he wants. It's quite clear that *he* wasn't in mourning for long.

'Maybe,' she agreed with enigmatic calm, 'but I would have thought it was what *I* had in mind that counted.' With

sudden heat she continued, 'I hope you've changed, Kyle.
You were very unforgiving then.' Before he could answer
she concluded, 'I'm not going to let you drive me away
from here, you know.'

'I've no intention of doing any such thing,' he said
coolly. 'How could I do that to a neighbour?'

'N-neighbour?' she stuttered.

'Yes. I signed a short lease for the vacant penthouse this
morning. Which reminds me that I have to go and start
moving my belongings. I'm leaving Graham Smith in
charge for the rest of the day.' With a brief nod he went.

The accommodation that Kyle was renting was high above
her own and prestigious to say the least, and as Hannah
made her way home at the end of the day all she could
think of was that, in spite of their hurtful conversation of
the afternoon, to some extent the barren years were over.

Kyle was back in her life again. Not as a lover, or even
a friend for that matter, but she was going to be seeing him
all the time during the next few months, and in spite of still
being in a state of shock at his sudden appearance, she'd
never felt more alive.

If she'd expected him to be hovering when she arrived
at the apartments she was to be disappointed. There was
no sign of him as she paid off the taxi, and when she looked
up at the windows of his new abode the curtains were still
drawn as they had been for weeks.

Her smile was wry as she put her key in the lock of her
own front door. She rarely saw any of the other occupants,
so why should he be any different?

'Hannah!' he said suddenly from behind, and she swung
round, startled, on the dimly lit landing. 'Sorry!' I didn't
mean to make you jump. I'm here to ask you out for a meal
in gratitude for getting me out of that hotel room.'

'There's no need,' she protested awkwardly, her poise

deserting her at the sudden encounter. 'I know how hard it can be to find accommodation in London.'

'How did you come across this place?' he asked as they faced each other in the shadows.

'A friend of mine from Manchester told me about it. Richard came to work in London ahead of me and he'd driven past it.'

She didn't know why she'd thrown Richard's name into the conversation. Maybe it was to let Kyle see that she wasn't entirely without a man.

Would Kyle care, though? So far he hadn't exactly been jumping for joy at meeting up with her again, and although he professed to be keen to hear what she'd been up to all the time they'd been apart, his only question had been about Paul.

It would seem that he *didn't* care as he merely commented, 'Good for you that he did.' He went on to ask, 'Have you eaten?'

'No. I was going to have something ghastly like a boiled egg.'

Hannah was cringing inwardly. What had possessed her to say that? He would think she was either playing the part of the lonely bedsit dweller or was just pathetic.

However, to her surprise he was laughing, a deep chuckle from low in his throat. Tears threatened. It was a sound she hadn't heard in many long years and yet it was as familiar now as it had been then.

'I think I can do better than that,' he said with the laughter still in him. 'Come on!' Taking her hand, he pressed the 'down' lift button.

His touch was like coming home, and Hannah began to tremble. If she wasn't careful she was going to make a fool of herself, she thought, but the moment was passing as the whirring of mechanism announced the lift had arrived and he let go of her hand.

*   *   *

Seated across from Kyle in a small restaurant nearby, Hannah wasn't aware how the gentle lighting turned her fair bob into a silver halo and the bright blue of her eyes into mysterious cobalt pools. The man opposite was, though, and it was Kyle's turn to question his motives.

He admitted to himself that he'd contrived this meeting. He'd watched for Hannah coming home, guessing that it would be at a similar time to the previous night, and had waylaid her on the landing without knowing exactly why.

There *had* been gratitude behind it. He'd been telling the truth when he'd said that. Finding somewhere to live could have been hellish without her help. He would be working long hours like the rest of them on the team and would have had little time for apartment-hunting.

But it wasn't just gratitude that had made him seek her out. There'd been a reason, just as there'd been a reason for wanting to clear the air about his son.

However, he could be presuming too much in thinking that Hannah might be interested in either himself or Ben. She'd already mentioned some guy called Richard and he'd heard Jack telling his copilot that he fancied her.

One thing was good, though. It didn't look as if anybody had been waiting for her behind the door she'd been about to unlock or she wouldn't be sitting opposite him now.

She was stunning, he thought in taut admiration. The pretty young trainee doctor he'd loved all that time ago was now a beautiful woman, doing an important job in what could often be hazardous circumstances.

His mouth twisted at the thought of how the fates had brought them together again. Maybe they thought that he'd played the part of the 'sinned against' long enough.

He'd been hurt and very angry when it had happened, but not without just cause. After being left to kick his heels on the sidelines for months while Hannah had comforted her brother-in-law, he'd found them in each other's arms and he'd gone berserk. So much so that he'd left the very same day for pastures new.

Yet now she was telling him that nothing had come of it. That the whinging Paul had married somebody else! How had she felt about that? he wondered. Had her heart been broken, too?

When he looked up she was watching him with questioning eyes. 'Where were your thoughts just then?' she asked quietly. 'With your son? In Australia? At the helipad?'

'None of those things,' he fibbed. 'I was wondering where my razor has got to during the move.'

They came out of the restaurant into a starlit night and as they walked side by side Hannah was so conscious of Kyle beside her that she felt he must surely hear the thundering of her heartbeats.

But he just shortened his long, easy stride to match hers and lapsed into a thoughtful silence until they reached the apartments that were now home to them both.

Back on the landing where he'd found her earlier they faced each other and Hannah wondered if he had any idea how much she wanted to keep him with her.

Whether it was because of the longing inside her, or merely exhaustion after a long day with the emergency services, she didn't know, but suddenly she found herself swaying on her feet.

The keen, dark eyes that didn't miss a thing had seen what was happening and he reached out for her and cradled her to him.

'What's the matter, Hannah?' he said softly. 'You're tired, aren't you? I should have realised and let you go to your bed, instead of tempting you outside to keep me company.'

She shook her head in wordless denial.

'So what is it, then?' he asked as his arms tightened around her.

'Is it this?' Lifting her face up to his, he kissed her lips fleetingly.

She nodded mutely and he did it again, and as her mouth sprang to life beneath his the years rolled away.

But maybe she was reading too much into it. Taking her key from her hand, he turned it in the lock and gently pushed her inside.

'Go to bed. I'll see you in the morning,' he said, and with a last backward look over his shoulder he headed towards the lift.

As she did as he'd suggested Hannah's mind was in chaos. It was still there! Incredibly, the flame that had burned so brightly all that time ago hadn't gone out. In those brief seconds in his arms she'd felt its warmth.

But then what had Kyle done? He'd broken into the moment with mundane considerations when she could have stayed there for ever.

Yet there was one consolation. 'I'll see you in the morning,' he'd said, and it was true. He would...and the day after...and the day after that, she thought, and what could be better than that? Whatever he did or said, Kyle was back in her life again.

CHAPTER THREE

WHEN they met the following morning Hannah was expecting there to be a new rapport between Kyle and herself after those moments outside her door, but there was little chance to follow it up.

The staff of the helicopter unit had barely had time to set foot on the premises before the alarm was sounding to say that somewhere inside the awakening city they were needed.

A message from the ambulance centre was coming through to alert them to a serious accident in Piccadilly Circus. A man flagging down a taxi had been hit by a young motorcyclist and both were badly hurt.

The helicopter had only just arrived and as those who were on the day's main response team ran to pick up their equipment, the two firefighters who were stationed at the helipad stood by.

Their function was to be there when the helicopter engines were switched on in case of fire and once that was satisfactorily accomplished Hannah, the doctor on duty, and the paramedic scrambled on board.

As they were about to take off into a clear morning sky the door opened and Kyle flung himself into the seat beside her. When she eyed him in surprise he said, 'I told you that I wasn't going to be sitting behind the desk all day.' Without further explanation he fixed his eyes on the approaching skyline.

The other member of the team was Pete Stubbs, who was now back on duty with fading bruises and a dressing on the partly healed cut.

'Just one more week and you'll be functional instead of the onlooker, eh, Hannah?' Pete said, as if he guessed that she wasn't entirely comfortable at that moment.

She smiled. He was a nice guy. In fact, all the team members were. The only one she wasn't so sure about was the man beside her. The man who this morning appeared to have reverted back to his usual aloof self if the uncompromising shoulder half turned away from her as he scanned the ground was anything to go by.

He was different. It wasn't liking that she felt for Kyle Templeton. It was something much deeper and yet, at this moment, rattled by his abrupt manner, she could have wished him miles away, instead of throwing her into confusion by his nearness.

When they'd first split up it had been agony to be without him and she'd searched for him far and wide...but sadly not as far as Australia.

The dreadful feeling of loss had gradually eased and for the last few years she'd been able to shut him from her mind for long periods. But two days ago that had all changed when she'd found him gazing down on her in a London street, looking tanned, trimly fit and even more heart-stopping than before.

She was both excited and dismayed to find that he still affected her, yet it was so. The excitement was because her personal life had been on hold for so long, and now the man responsible for that had come back from the limbo he'd disappeared into all that time ago.

The dismay stemmed from the feeling that to all intents and purposes she was still the 'unforgiven'.

All right, Kyle had made a friendly gesture last night when he'd invited her to eat with him, but he'd explained why. He was grateful to have somewhere to live and probably didn't want to eat alone.

When she'd started to wilt he must have felt responsible

and had acted accordingly, but on finding out that he was giving the wrong signals he'd retreated.

'I'm going to land between those two office blocks behind the main shopping area,' Jack called over his shoulder as they hovered over the heads of the workbound masses. 'It's the nearest I can get.'

Kyle nodded his agreement and within seconds they were down. As they scrambled out they didn't have far to look for the scene of the accident. The traffic was snarled up for as far as the eye could see, and the taxi driver was leaning against his cab, his head in his hands.

His would-be passenger was lying in the road. While Pete and their own man from the unit ran towards them, Hannah and Kyle sprinted to where the motorcyclist lay in a crumpled heap beside his similarly affected bike.

As they approached a by-stander said, 'This guy hit the other fellow and then with his bike out of control crashed into these iron railings at an entrance to the underground. He's been unconscious ever since it happened,' he informed them. 'The crash helmet protected his head but there could be neck and spinal injuries.'

Kyle was already bending over him and as Hannah crouched beside him he said urgently, 'I don't like the looks of him. He checked the man's breathing and his face tightened in alarm. 'No function!' he said urgently. 'We're going to have to resuscitate him. I'll do the mouth-to-mouth while you apply cardiac compression. OK?'

She nodded as the bedlam caused by the accident went on around her. There was the screeching of police sirens, the tooting of horns in cars brought to a halt by it, and the noise from the crowds that congregated so quickly at the slightest sign of anything out of the ordinary in a city street.

As they worked side by side all Hannah's earlier annoyances fled in the urgency of the moment. This is what it's all about, she told herself. Getting here! A fast response to an emergency! And with one of the country's top men in A and E, it makes everything else in one's life seem unimportant.

When the youth began to breathe again their eyes met and he smiled briefly. 'Well done, Dr Morgan. The next thing is to get this young fellow fixed up with a collar and onto a spinal board. We'll get moving before any more complications set in.

'But first I must check on our other patient to see which of the two is the more serious and will need to be airlifted, while the other is transferred by ambulance when it gets through. Stay with him,' he ordered, and went running to where Pete and the paramedic were still treating the other man.

'He's badly shaken with a broken ankle and arm,' he reported when he came back, 'but that appears to be all. So this fellow is our priority. You can supervise him being stretchered to the helicopter while I ring the hospital with details of his injuries. Pete can follow on with the other casualty.'

When the young motorcyclist had been admitted to the hospital Kyle said, 'I've got to get back and so has the Eurocopter. Pete and his assistant are tied up here for the time being so I'll send a car for them. You can travel back with me.'

'Yes, all right,' she agreed meekly, knowing that she didn't have much choice.

'And so where is that brother-in-law of yours these days?' Kyle asked suddenly as they became airborne.

'I've no idea,' she told him calmly, as if the question was of no consequence. 'At the time he remarried, Paul was living in the Midlands. I've no idea where he is now.'

'Who did he marry?'

'His secretary.'

'So when did you last see him?'

'Six, maybe seven years ago.'

'So you split up soon after I left?'

'No, we didn't! There was nothing to split up from! You would have found that out if you'd stayed long enough to listen to me,' she told him coldly. 'Paul was totally distraught when my twin died. I not only had my own grief to contend with, but had to support him as well. I knew you weren't happy about the time I was spending with him, but what could I do? Leave him to wallow in misery? He was threatening suicide half of the time.

'And do you have to be so nosy anyway?' she flared. 'I don't know how you have the nerve to start questioning me in this manner. You forfeited any right to interfere in my life when you went storming off like a cuckolded husband.'

'Can you blame me?' he said through gritted teeth. 'You were spending every moment of your free time with him, and where at first I understood, after all those months it became a bit much.'

'I know,' she agreed in a quieter tone. 'In the end I realised he was manipulating me. Pulling my strings to keep me by his side.'

'I don't know about that,' he said grimly, 'but that was some clinch I found you both in.'

'On Paul's part maybe. It was like he had me in a vice. His excuse afterwards was that I was so like Janine that he couldn't resist me.'

'That was a sick thing to say.'

'Yes, it was and I told him so, but, of course, you weren't there to listen. You always were too quick to jump to conclusions.'

'Maybe I was,' he admitted with a twisted smile. 'And now? Do I still appear to be the same?'

'I'll have to wait and see, won't I?' she replied smoothly,

with an uneasy feeling inside that last night it had been she who'd been guilty of that.

He lowered his voice. 'I think we've both changed since then, Hannah. You aren't as soft and malleable as you were then and I'm more tolerant.'

'Huh! Thank you for that!' she hooted. 'Maybe in my case it's been that absence has made the heart grow "harder". Which wouldn't be likely to occur in yours as your heart was like a stone from the start.'

He was actually laughing. 'Past tense. Since Ben was born I've been soft as putty.'

Hannah caught her breath. It hurt to know that he had a child that she hadn't borne him, but there was nothing she could do about it. The chance to give him children had been taken from her.

He was touching her arm and as usual the contact made her blood warm. 'Well done this morning anyway. We got the lad to hospital in record time. So let's hope that there is good news on him soon and on the unfortunate pedestrian.'

Hannah nodded. The motorcyclist and the man who'd dashed into his path could have been killed in the accident at Piccadilly Circus. Even so they would be facing long and painful treatment.

And what were she and Kyle doing? Playing at cat and mouse? Opening up old wounds that were best left alone. It was over and done with. Only the present mattered, unnerving though it might be.

In the days that followed a pattern developed between them, based on a cool politeness when on the job and a guarded sort of neighbourliness if they met in or around the apartment block. It seemed as if the brief yet searching talk they'd had on the helicopter the third day after Kyle's arrival had set the seal on future relations. Or the lack of them.

The fact that she was all the time achingly aware of him was hard to cope with, but Hannah had a gut feeling that any forward move had to come from Kyle. If it came from her she would never be sure of what his feelings were.

When she sat alone in the evenings she was acutely conscious that he was up there, high above her, doing his own thing just as she was doing hers, and there was no comfort in it. It was a strange feeling. Just as it was when they caught the same train on the underground. Or were thrown together on the job.

Hannah knew that he went to see his son on his days off.

That he set off in the early hours and returned very late and that he was always very sombre the following day.

On one occasion she asked, 'Is everything all right with Ben?'

He observed her with surprised dark eyes. 'Yes. He's settled down famously. Why do you ask?'

'It's just that you're always very quiet when you've been to see him.'

His smile was wry. 'I find it hard to leave Ben every time I see him. I want him here with me in London. But first I have to find a suitable house. I don't want him caged up in an apartment or suchlike. I'm relieved that he's happy at my parents' place but...'

'You want him with you?'

'Correct.' He hunched broad shoulders. 'I miss him, Hannah. I suppose I should have taken a job in gentler surroundings if I was intent on coming back to England. Maybe in the same area as my mum and dad, so that we could all be together.'

His glance took in the busy operations room and the bright outline of the helicopter, and he went on to say, 'But this place is me. It's where I belong. I've done this kind of work for a long time and it's a very rewarding occupation.'

She wasn't able to argue with that. They all felt the same, but Kyle was the best, and in only a short time Smitty, Pete Stubbs and David, who was finishing on the coming Friday, all acknowledged his skills and dedication.

'And,' he went on in a totally different kind of voice, 'if I hadn't come to this place I wouldn't have met you again, would I?'

'Would that have mattered?' she asked with rising colour. 'I can't see me ever competing with Ben.'

'Two people. Two different compartments,' he told her enigmatically, and if he'd been intending to elaborate on that she wasn't to hear it as the alarm was sounding. Another emergency was waiting for them.

Hannah had finished her probation and was as functional as the rest of them now, taking her own call-outs with a paramedic to assist and sometimes with Kyle himself on board when the mood took him or he felt that an extra pair of hands was going to be needed.

On those occasions she was always tense. Not sure if he was there because she was so recent an addition to the team that she needed watching, or whether it was coincidence that it was nearly always her emergency responses he attached himself to.

Jack had noticed and when she'd refused to go out with him a fourth time he'd said good-naturedly, 'It's not Templeton, is it? I've seen the way he looks at you.'

'No. It's not. I'm too tired to go anywhere when I've finished here,' she'd told him and he'd had to be satisfied with that.

David Wainright was taking up a consultancy in one of the London hospitals on the following Monday, and on the Friday night, once darkness had settled over the city, they all went to a nearby wine bar to have a farewell drink with him.

Everyone was there—the operations officer, the firemen based at the helipad, the paramedics and, of course, the doctors.

Hannah was conscious of being the only woman present and she'd brought a smart, black silk trouser suit to change into which showed up darkly against her silver fairness.

From the moment of seeing her in it Jack had been hovering, as beneath the soft lighting of the wine bar she looked even more desirable.

A far cry indeed from the doctor in her vivid surgical suit, who earlier that day had attended a woman dragged from the Thames and a barrow boy who'd been lying unconscious on the pavement with a cracked skull after an altercation with a fellow trader.

Kyle hadn't been with her on those occasions as she'd frantically resuscitated the half-drowned woman and later managed to get the injured man to Charing Cross in record time, and she hadn't known whether to be glad or sorry.

It wasn't so much that he made her nervous. She was quite capable of handling those sort of emergencies, but it was the same whenever they were together in whatever circumstances. She was so aware of him she could hardly breathe.

When she turned he was beside her, glass in hand, eyes cool and inscrutable, and she wondered if he'd noticed that she was dressed up for the occasion.

If he had he wasn't letting on. 'Are we going to share a taxi later?' he asked.

'Er…yes…if you want,' she said coolly, as the hope that he might have come to talk about something other than travelling arrangements died at birth.

'Let me know when you're ready to go, then, and I'll ring for one.' As she nodded dumbly he moved away.

Feeling unaccountably miffed at his attitude Hannah sauntered across to where Jack was chatting up the girl behind the bar and, linking her arm in his, smiled up at him.

If Kyle's attention was an unattainable sort of thing, not so this man's. He was immediately tuned in and for the rest of the evening she let him monopolise her.

'Does our arrangement still stand? Or is Krasner taking you home?' Kyle said abruptly as the party began to make a move towards departure.

'It still stands,' she told him calmly, knowing that if she let Jack take her home he wouldn't want to leave...and would read something into it that wasn't there.

'Come on, then, or he'll be thinking that I'm muscling in on him.'

That will be the day! Hannah thought grimly.

After a quick farewell to David, Kyle hustled her out onto the pavement, and when she turned she could see Jack through the window, looking over the remaining members of the party with a puzzled eye. It seemed as if he hadn't noticed her rapid exit or he would have been out there, staking his claim.

Kyle had followed her glance and as a taxi pulled in at the kerb he said drily, 'You've still time to change your mind.'

Hannah shook her head. Suddenly she was very tired and not without cause. It had been a long day. Up at six-thirty, on the tube at seven, and taking her place along with the rest of them at seven-thirty. Now it was close to midnight and she knew that her exhaustion was mental as much as physical...and Kyle Templeton was to blame for that.

If only she knew what was in his mind. He was easy enough to understand when it came to the job. He'd not concealed his feelings about Ben. But he was rarely forthcoming with regard to herself.

Maybe he saw what had happened in the past as too long ago to even think about, she thought as they settled themselves into the back of the cab. Or if he did still have reservations about her, perhaps he'd decided that he would have to grin and bear it until her six months were up.

He was gazing through the taxi window with his head turned away from her and Hannah had a sudden crazy desire to touch his cheek with the tips of her fingers. She was actually reaching out to him when he turned, and as their eyes met her hand fell away.

He'd seen the movement.

'What?'

She shook her head.

'Nothing.'

The driver pulled up in front of their apartment block at that moment and those seconds together in the darkness of the cab were over.

As Kyle settled the fare Hannah prepared to follow him onto the pavement, but her heel caught in the hemline of the silk trousers and she lurched forward. She would have fallen if he hadn't caught her in his arms, and as the taxi sped away his hold tightened.

She looked up at him. 'Thanks for that,' she said breathlessly. 'For a moment I thought I was going to end up in a heap.'

He didn't speak, just continued to hold her and she became still. As the seconds passed Hannah prayed that he couldn't feel her trembling. She didn't want to move out of the circle of his arms, but neither did she want him to think that he had only to beckon and she would be there.

When she could stand it no longer she breathed his name and like a man in a dream Kyle shook his head as if to clear it. Then he held her away from him so that he could see her face beneath the streetlights.

This time, as their eyes locked, they were so tuned in to

each other's need she felt as if her legs would give way beneath her.

'Shall we see if it's as good as it was before?' he said as he put a finger under her chin and tilted her face up to his.

Hannah stiffened. 'Do you have to bring up the past, Kyle? It's gone. Done with, as far as I'm concerned.'

'So you've no regrets?'

'I didn't say that.'

It was hardly the moment to tell him that she'd lived on a diet of regret for years and all because she'd been too malleable in the hands of a grieving widower…and he, Kyle, had been a lover with a very short fuse.

'Right. So let's say that this is for old times' sake, shall we?' Placing his mouth on hers, he kissed her with the hungry intensity that she remembered so well.

They drew apart at last and as they did so sanity returned.

'That should have been for the present,' she whispered. 'Not the past.'

He raised a sardonic eyebrow. 'Is that so?' and to her chagrin he glanced at his watch. 'Goodnight, Hannah Morgan. If we don't make tracks it will be time for the morning rush hour before we've even hit the sack.'

Hannah nodded bleakly and, leaving him standing on the pavement, hurtled through the doors of the apartment block. Without waiting for the lift, she went up the stairs two at a time.

Once inside her own flat she leant against the door and stayed there until her heart stopped hammering. Then she walked slowly to the sofa and eased herself down amongst its soft cushions.

She could still feel his mouth on hers, his possessive hold and the magic of being where she belonged after the long fast. But Kyle hadn't said anything to make her think that he still cared. For all she knew he'd seen her as a temporary diversion, and tomorrow they would be back in routine.

They were. The following day he was brisk, businesslike, the man at the top. All of those things as the day got under way. If Kyle had any lingering thoughts about the night before he wasn't showing it.

It was Graham Smith's turn to lead the major response team today, while Hannah and Pete Stubbs would deal with any secondary calls that came in if the helicopter was already in service. In those instances an ambulance was used and consequently there was a longer time factor in getting the patient to hospital.

By lunchtime the Eurocopter had been called out twice, which had meant a busy morning for Graham and his team but for Pete and herself there had been time to relax for once.

'You made a quick getaway last night,' Jack had said when she'd arrived early that morning. 'I don't bite, you know. I believe you went home with the chief.'

'Yes, I did,' she'd told him with a conciliatory smile. 'It was an economical arrangement as we live in the same apartment block.'

He'd stared at her with mouth agape. 'How come?'

'When he first came he asked me if I knew of a vacant apartment anywhere and I told him I did, that there was one in the complex where I live.'

His eyes had narrowed. 'Why ask you?'

So far no one on the unit knew that she and Kyle had met before. Perhaps this was the moment to make it known, as if it ever did come out there would be raised eyebrows at the way they'd kept quiet about it.

'We know each other from way back.'

'Really?'

She smiled at his amazement. 'Yes, "really", Jack. So you see why he—'

'Has such an interest in you?'

'Huh! That'll be the day.'

'Don't you believe it, my child,' he said with his good humour returning. 'That guy is not immune to your charms. And speaking of those, neither are the rest of us.'

The first alarm sounded at that moment so she was saved from any more of the pilot's banter.

In the middle of the morning as Hannah and Pete were chatting over a mug of coffee, Kyle appeared at her side. 'Have you got a moment, Hannah?' he asked quietly. As she got to her feet, he added, 'In the office, if you don't mind.'

He closed the door once she was seated and she was tempted to remind him of what he'd said on that first day…that just because they were acquainted it didn't mean that they would be closeted in his office all the time.

When he'd settled himself behind his desk he observed her without speaking and she said quickly, 'I take it that I'm in trouble of some sort. If it's anything to do with last night don't even mention it! What I do outside working hours is not your concern…even if you are involved.'

'It's funny that you should say that,' he said as the vestige of a smile tugged at his mouth. 'It's what you do outside working hours that I want to discuss.'

'You really have got a nerve!' she told him angrily.

'I'm afraid that you'll think that even more when you hear what I have to say,' he said blandly.

'So what is it?'

'My parents are bringing Ben up to London tomorrow but they can't stay. 'I'm anxious to see my son, as you can imagine, and intended spending the day with him, but something's come up which means that I won't be available for part of the morning.'

Light was dawning and her spirits lifting. 'So, as it's my day off, you're asking me to look after him for you. Is that it?'

He swallowed hard. 'Er…yes…that's about it, Hannah. Would you?'

Her face lit up. 'Yes, of course. I'd love to. Let me know where and when I have to pick him up and what he likes to do.'

He'd been frowning before but now his brow was clearing. 'Thank you Hannah. I really appreciate this. I'll bring Ben round to your place if that's all right?'

Hannah nodded. Of course it was. At this moment everything was all right. Kyle was going to trust her with his son. Maybe she'd moved up a peg, and for the rest of the day she was planning where she would take Ben and what they would do.

Hannah didn't get the chance to speak to Kyle again during the rest of the day. He was bogged down with showing some VIPs around the operations room and when they'd gone he went out with Graham on yet another emergency. When they got back the rest of them were on the point of leaving and he just bade her a brief goodnight.

If she thought that the arrangements for the following day had been a bit vague Hannah consoled herself with the thought that at least he had asked her to help.

For once he wasn't keeping her at arm's length. But was it anything to go by? The night before they'd been in each other's arms and for her it had been like coming home after a long banishment, but what had it meant to Kyle? He'd soon backed off.

Before making herself the nightly snack that went under the heading of 'dinner', Hannah took off her working clothes and went under the shower.

As the water's rejuvenating spray eased away the grime

and tensions of a day amongst the rooftops she said to herself, 'Live one day at a time.'

If he was nothing else, Kyle Templeton was full of surprises, and just as long as they were pleasant ones like tomorrow's arrangement...and those bone-melting moments the night before in the light of the streetlamps, she would go along with them.

CHAPTER FOUR

AT HALF past ten Hannah was watching the end of a play on television and fighting off sleep at the same time when her doorbell rang, and immediately her drowsiness fell away.

Visitors were rare, especially at this time of night, and her heartbeat quickened. She'd put on a nightdress and a lightweight robe after her shower and having to open the door to a caller in such attire was the last thing she'd expected.

There was only one person that it was likely to be and he'd left it a bit late if he was calling to discuss the next day. Before she could get to the door the bell rang again, and when she checked to see who it was Hannah saw that her assumption had been wrong. Richard was standing on the mat.

'I hope I haven't got you out of bed,' he said stiffly when she opened the door to him.

Hannah shook her head as disappointment washed over her. Richard was the last person she wanted to see, but he was here and she supposed that for old times' sake she ought to ask him in.

'I was just about to turn in,' she said as she stepped back to let him pass. 'It's been a long day. What can I do for you?'

She was trying to be pleasant, but he was already seating himself. Seeing him sprawled against her cushions, it made her realise just how much she'd wanted the late-night caller to be Kyle.

'It's what I can do for you.' he said with a patronising smile.

'Oh?'

'Yes. I've won a holiday for two in Barbados and am offering you the chance to join me. I've been dining out with some of the folk from work and was on my way home when I thought of you as a possible candidate for sharing in my good fortune.'

Hannah sighed. He was thick-skinned this one! They hadn't seen each other in weeks and on the last occasion when they had she'd made it clear that she'd wanted nothing else to do with him.

If Richard was expecting her to fall upon him and say 'Yes! Please!' he was mistaken. But she supposed there had to be some goodwill behind the offer and so she told him politely, 'I'm sorry, Richard, but if you remember I did say that last time we met that our acquaintance had run its course.'

He was staring at her in disbelief and it was all she could do not to smile.

'You don't want to come?' he spluttered.

'I'm afraid so.'

He was on his feet.

'Right. Suit yourself. I thought you'd be—'

'Falling over myself to take you up on the offer?'

'Something like that…yes.'

She could almost pity him for the size of his ego. Letting him off lightly, she said, 'I'm sure that there must be lots of other women who would jump at the chance of holidaying with you.'

For a second his superior façade crumbled and he said with a wry smile, 'If I were more easy to get on with, perhaps.'

He was at the door, ready to make his exit, and as he stepped out on to the corridor Hannah felt sorry for him.

Giving him a quick hug and a fleeting kiss on the cheek, she said softly, 'If you've worked that out, you're almost there, Richard. Good luck with the holiday.' As he walked slowly towards the lift she went back inside and closed the door.

It was gone ten o'clock before Kyle left the helipad. It had been as the sun was setting in a midsummer sky that he and Graham Smith had returned from that last response of the day, and he'd been fretting ever since because he hadn't made proper arrangements for the next day with Hannah.

He could have phoned her, but it seemed churlish not to speak to her in person when they lived so near to each other. He'd been truly grateful at the way she'd so willingly agreed to do what he'd asked. After all it was her day off and, after a week on the helipad, they were all ready for a rest.

A quick word before he turned in for the night was what he was intending and as the lift deposited him on the floor where she lived he was about to stride across to her door when it opened.

He halted. A man of a similar age to himself was coming out and as Kyle moved back into the shadows on the landing he saw Hannah framed in the doorway behind him.

When her visitor turned to say his farewells she hugged him to her, with her lips against his cheek, and with the movement the neck of her flimsy robe fell away, revealing a smooth shoulder and the cleft between her breasts.

Kyle was writhing inwardly. It wasn't the clinging brother-in-law this time. Though the fellow looked a similar type, he thought irritably. But as it was none of his business who Hannah spent her free time with, there was nothing he could do about it.

Once the unknown visitor had gone and she'd shut her door, he walked slowly up the stairs to his own apartment.

He didn't want to have to face her, not having just witnessed the departure of lover boy. That seemed an apt description after an eyeful of what Hannah was, or was not, wearing.

Hannah had just slid between the sheets when the phone rang, and this time it was Kyle. 'Sorry to ring so late, Hannah,' he said flatly.

'It's all right. I wasn't asleep.'

Don't I know it, he thought grimly.

'It's about tomorrow.'

'Yes. I thought it might be,' she replied, and he could tell that she was smiling, which could have been for a variety of reasons and none of them anything to do with him.

'Mum and Dad will be in London by ten so I'll bring Ben round to your place about half past ten. Is that OK?' he questioned in the same flat tone.

'Yes,' she said immediately. 'And, Kyle…'

'What?'

'Get some rest, or you'll be too flaked out to enjoy your time with Ben.'

'I'll try,' he promised abruptly. 'Goodnight, Hannah.'

When he'd gone off the line she stood looking into the receiver. He'd sounded odd. Was he all right?'

On impulse she dialled his number.

'Yes?' he barked.

'It's me again, Kyle,' she explained. 'Are you all right? You sounded a bit strange when you were on before.'

'Of course I'm bloody all right!' he bellowed into her ear. 'Don't fuss, Hannah.'

Her face flamed as she replaced the handset. If that was all the thanks she got for being concerned over him, he could get lost!

Kyle groaned as the line went dead. Could he do anything right where she was concerned? It was clear that any feelings she'd had for him were long since dead, and the fact that she had other men in her life wasn't surprising.

Hannah was beautiful, a good doctor and kind with it. What more could any man ask? What more could he ask? That he hadn't wasted the last eight years for no reason? Because if he had he was some fool.

When the bell rang the following morning Hannah was ready. In jeans and a comfortable cotton shirt and with trainers on her feet, she was geared for action.

She'd decided to take Ben to the zoo if Kyle approved. It would be too much to fit in during a couple of hours, but she hoped that he might decide to join them when the meeting was over.

'Here we are, Hannah,' Kyle said with what she immediately recognised as false heartiness.

He looked down at the small fair-haired boy holding tightly onto his hand. 'And this is Ben.'

Hannah went across and knelt beside him. 'Hello, Ben,' she sad softly. 'I'm Hannah, and I'm sure that we're going to have lots of fun getting to know each other.'

He didn't answer, just nodded and then buried his face against his father.

Kyle was observing her over his head and he said quietly, 'He'll be all right once he gets to know you.'

She was smiling. Nothing was going to throw her today. 'Yes, of course,' she agreed. Turning her attention back to the boy, she said, 'I thought we might go to the zoo. Would you like that?'

He fixed her with one eye, while the other remained hidden against Kyle's shirtsleeve.

'Mmm,' he murmured.

'Yes, please, if you don't mind, young man!' Kyle said with an apologetic glance in her direction. 'You're not going to see much of the zoo in the time I'll be at the meeting.'

'I thought that maybe you could meet us there,' Hannah said hesitantly.

He was eyeing her blankly. 'Er…yes…I suppose so…if you've got nothing else planned.'

It was an innocuous enough remark but she sensed there was something behind it. What did he think she was involved in on her day off? A mad social whirl!

Usually it was shopping in the morning, lunch somewhere and then a film in the evening. Pleasant up to a point, but doing the same thing every week did take the excitement out of it.

'I haven't got anything else planned,' she assured him. 'So where shall we meet?'

'By the lion house?'

'Yes. that will be fine.'

He was looking at his watch. 'I have to go, Hannah.' With a quick hug for Ben he prepared to leave. When she went with him to the door he said in a low voice, 'Keep your eye on him, will you? Mum said he was very listless on the train and that isn't Ben. It's probably because they had an early start but you never know with kids.'

'I will. Rest assured,' she told him, and as he went striding off there were tears on her lashes. He was a strange mixture. Clever, loyal, passionate, a devoted father.

From the looks of it he was happy to be a single parent to his son. A lot of men would have had second thoughts about that sort of responsibility. But, then, they weren't Kyle Templeton, were they? Yet when it came to herself he had a low tolerance threshold.

When she went back into the sitting room Ben was curled up on the sofa, fast asleep, and she thought whimsically, So much for getting to know him.

Yet there was plenty of time. The speed with which he'd

gone to sleep was a bit unusual, but obviously he was tired after the journey and the early start.

Dragging a tired child around the zoo would be no fun for either of them. She would let him have his sleep out, and then they would go.

An hour went by and Hannah knew if she didn't rouse Ben soon Kyle could be there before them. But when she bent over him she saw that his face was flushed. When she felt his brow he was burning.

He opened his eyes at that moment and croaked, 'Can I have a drink, Hannah?'

'Yes, of course, darling,' she said, and hurried into the kitchen.

When she got back he was sitting up. 'My head hurts and the light is too bright, Hannah,' he sobbed. 'I want my daddy!'

She rang Kyle on his mobile and had barely finished telling him what was happening before he said he was on his way. When she went back to Ben he was worse. He was having trouble swallowing, as if the membranes of his throat were affected. This was a nightmare, she thought desperately.

What would he think when he knew that the moment he'd left his son in her care it had all gone wrong? She loved the man. Always had. She couldn't bear to think that he would never again trust her with his child.

'Hannah!' Ben was croaking. 'Where's daddy? My throat hurts as well as my head.'

She was trying to get him to have a sip of water but he pushed it away. The purple rash was still there, and as she eyed it thoughtfully she wondered.

'Ben,' Hannah said softly, 'do you know what an allergy is?'

'Mmm. Grandma says its something that doesn't like you.' he wailed.

'And do you know of anything that doesn't like you?'

He shook his head without speaking and she had to be satisfied with that.

Hearing a noise outside she ran to the window and was relieved to see Kyle flinging himself out of a car.

When she opened the door Kyle was coming up the stairs two at a time, his face grey with anxiety. 'Where is he?' he asked as he pushed past her.

'In the bedroom,' she whispered.

By the time he got to the bed where she'd laid the sick child he'd switched from the mantle of the anxious father to that of the doctor and was making a swift examination of his little patient.

Hannah noticed that he hadn't asked for her opinion but, like it or not, he was going to get it.

'Is Ben allergic to anything?'

'Er…what?' Kyle asked absently as he took Ben's hot little hand in his, and then it registered what she'd said.

'Allergy!' he exclaimed. 'You might have something there, Hannah, darling! Mum mentioned that Ben had been stung by a bee yesterday, so she took him into the surgery.'

'And they gave him an injection,' she finished off for him.

'Yes! Indeed! If it's an allergy from that, an antidote will do the trick. Let's keep our fingers crossed that it is.'

He picked Ben up in his arms. 'Let's be on our way—and if you're right, Hannah, I'll love you for ever.'

Words! she thought wryly as they went. But she'd liked the sound of them.

She'd ached to go with them but was aware that Kyle might not want her to tag along. And once Ben's grandparents knew about his condition there would be enough of them by his bedside without casual acquaintances. She would have to wait, and pray that there would soon be some news.

Pete rang her later on behalf of Kyle to confirm that Ben had been admitted and tests were being done to see if her surmise was correct. It would be some time before they had any answers.

'Kyle says he'll be in touch as soon as he has any news,' he told her and then commiserated, 'What a way to spend your day off. Having someone else's precious child go sick on you to that extent.'

She shuddered. 'Don't remind me. It was a nightmare. But thank goodness Kyle got Ben to hospital so quickly.'

'Yes, indeed.' She heard the alarm go off in the background. 'Must go I'm afraid, Hannah.'

It was late afternoon when the phone rang again and Hannah couldn't get to it quickly enough.

It was Kyle and he wasn't concerned with the niceities. 'You were right, Hannah,' he said when she answered. 'Ben is allergic to the injection that my parent's GP gave him yesterday.'

Relief was making her feel weak and she didn't answer immediately. 'Did you hear what I said?' he asked, as if he thought her silence strange.

'Yes,' she breathed. 'It's just that I've been sitting here for hours imagining the worst. Has Ben been given the antidote to clear up the reaction to the jab?'

'Of course,' he said briskly, 'and he's already feeling some improvement. I'm sorry I haven't rung you before but I've had my parents to deal with as well. I managed to contact them with the news and they decided to come and see him.'

His voice had lightened and there was laughter in it as he said, 'And by the way, Ben thinks you're wonder woman for looking after him. I won't be able to get a look in the next time he wants to play doctors. I can see him insisting that we send for you.'

'I'm only too glad I did,' she told him as unshed tears thickened the words. 'I've never seen anything come on so quickly. One moment we were ready to be off to the zoo, and the next Ben was so poorly I couldn't believe it. I felt dreadful because you'd only just left him in my care.'

'There's no need to feel like that,' Kyle said, and she sensed that he was retreating behind the barrier of reserve he could erect within seconds. 'I'm only too sorry that you've had all this hassle with me and mine.'

Hannah was about to tell him that she didn't mind. That nothing mattered as long as Ben was going to be all right. It would have been wonderful if she'd also felt that she could tell him that, given time, she could love the boy as much as she loved his father. But he was already closing up against her. For what reason she didn't know. Unless something she'd said had reminded him not to get too involved with a two-timing ex-girlfriend.

'I have to go, Hannah,' he said, breaking into her sober reasoning. 'They're going to keep Ben in for a couple of days. So I won't be up amongst the rooftops with you for a while. Mum and Dad are going to use my penthouse until he's well enough to take him back to their place.'

'Yes. I see,' she said quickly, adding, before he could ring off, 'Is it all right if I pop in to see Ben?'

'Er…yes…if you get the chance,' he said slowly, as if she'd taken him by surprise. 'And now I really must go. He's been asleep, but is now showing signs of rousing and I don't want him to find me missing when he wakes.'

As Kyle returned to Ben's bedside his mother looked at him questioningly. Feeling that he should give an explanation for his brief absence, Kyle said, 'I've just been phoning my doctor friend, Hannah Morgan, to let her know how Ben is. It was most unfortunate that she should have been responsible for Ben when he was taken ill.'

'Yes, indeed,' his mother agreed. 'Does the lady work in the emergency services with you?'

He nodded. When the two of them had been in love all that time ago he'd been away from home and his parents had known little about what he'd done in his spare time, so the name wouldn't be familiar to them.

But his mother soon picked up on things and if he wasn't careful she would tune in to the turmoil inside him every time Hannah's name was mentioned…and that was a minor turbulence compared to what he was like when he was in her presence.

He'd harked back a couple of times to the disastrous day when he'd found her in a passionate embrace with her recently bereaved brother-in-law, and she'd immediately flared up at him bringing back the hurtful past.

Hannah hadn't been repentant or embarrassed on those occasions. She had been coldly indignant, and now, because he had this awful feeling that he'd been a bit too previous when he'd stormed off and left her in jealous pride, it was the last thing he wanted to talk about.

Yet whatever his own feelings for her were, Hannah had been a hit with Ben. As soon as he'd begun to feel better he had asked, 'When is Hannah coming to see me?'

'I don't know,' Kyle had told him, but I'm sure she will soon.'

The driver of a car approaching Great Cumberland Place had lost control of the vehicle and run into a solitary woman waiting at a bus stop.

The call-out had come in the middle of the next morning and as it was Hannah's turn to lead the main team of the day it was she and an assistant paramedic who ran to climb aboard the Eurocopter.

As they flew over the green expanse of Hyde Park and then Marble Arch towering above the bustling crowds of

Oxford Street, Hannah felt her pulses quickening. What were they going to be faced with this time? she wondered.

With his seemingly effortless skill Jack landed the Eurocopter in a small square near to the accident scene, and the moment they had touched down Hannah and the paramedic were off. They pushed their way through the gaping crowds to where the man sat trapped behind the steering-wheel of his car, and the unfortunate woman lay amongst the shattered glass of both car and bus shelter.

Police were already there, coping with the two casualties and a steadily accumulating traffic build-up.

'A witness states that the guy in the car was driving along at a reasonable pace when he suddenly slumped over the wheel and the car careered into the woman at the bus stop,' one of the policemen said.

Hannah nodded and hurried to where the injured woman was lying on her side in what was left of the bus shelter. The paramedic attended to the driver of the car, only to report back that there were no signs of life.

Middle-aged, and dressed in a brightly coloured sari, the woman was bleeding heavily from the back of her head and shoulders.

It seemed as if she had taken the impact of the car full on, not having had time to move. The injuries she had sustained were from being lifted onto the bonnet of the vehicle and then flung off against the back of the bus shelter as it had splintered around her.

'I'm going to cut her clothing away so I can see just what damage has been done,' Hannah told the hovering policemen. 'Will you move the onlookers back to give us some privacy?' As she looked into a pair of dark, terrified eyes she added, 'Ask everyone to make less noise. What has happened to this lady is bad enough without all this shouting going on around her.

'There appear to be leg fractures from where the bumper

hit her full on, but the upper part of the body was saved from more serious injury because it was carried along on the bonnet,' she went on. 'I'm most concerned about the gashes to her head and shoulders where she was slammed up against the metal frame of the shelter. What is your name?' she asked gently of the injured woman, but the reply wasn't coherent enough for Hannah to understand.

One thing Hannah did know was that the woman needed prompt treatment—skull X-rays, stitches in the many deep cuts and the broken bones needed setting.

As she put antiseptic pads over the areas that were bleeding the most and supervised the patient being strapped to a stretcher to prevent any jolting of her leg bones, Hannah was already ringing the trauma team at the nearest hospital.

It was only as they became airborne that she remembered that little Ben was in there and the thought came that, given the chance, she would pop in to see him.

The chance did present itself. As the injured woman was wheeled quickly away to have her injuries assessed Hannah sprinted down to the children's ward, calling at the hospital shop on the way.

She'd told Jack that she wanted to visit Ben and he'd told her to go ahead. If an emergency was relayed out to him he would seek her out.

The little boy was alone when she found him, sitting up in bed looking at a picture book, and at first he didn't recognise her in the bright surgical suit.

But when she settled herself on a chair by his bed and smiled across at him he cried, 'Hannah! It's you!' adding with typical childish directness, 'When can I have the treat?'

'As soon as you're better,' she said laughingly. 'When you've got rid of your spots.'

He immediately lifted his pyjama jacket and said stoutly, 'They've gone.'

The blotches were certainly fading, but she wouldn't describe them as 'gone'. However, she wasn't going to argue.

'Where's Daddy, and Grandma and Grandad?' she asked, having expected to face the full family Templeton when she got there.

'Daddy has gone to see when he can take me home,' he informed her, 'and Grandma and Grandad have gone to his flat to have a nap.'

'I see.'

She did. She saw that at any moment Kyle would be back and she couldn't wait to see him again. She'd managed without him for eight long years and now…now she hated to be away from him for a couple of days.

'Hannah!' Kyle exclaimed as he came striding back into the ward. 'How do you come to be here? You're on duty.'

She stiffened. What did he mean by that? Was it a reprimand? Or merely statement of fact?

'Er…yes…' she agreed. 'I am. We've just brought an accident victim in. They're attending to her now and I thought that while I was in the hospital I would look in on Ben. Jack will come to find me if we get another emergency.'

Her pleasure at being with them both was being wiped out by the feeling that she'd had to explain her presence. As if she were committing a misdemeanour of some sort. Surely Kyle knew that she was fully aware of the demands of the job? Or perhaps his greeting had been less than cordial because he associated her with disruption in his life.

Whatever he was thinking, there was no lack of enthusiasm on his son's part as Ben said excitedly, 'Hannah has come to see me in the helicopter, and she says I can still have my treat when I'm better.'

Kyle ruffled the boy's fair mop with an affectionate hand, but his glance was on Hannah as he said, 'They've just said that we can take Ben home this afternoon, so Mum and Dad will be taking him back to the Cotswolds tomorrow.'

'Fair enough,' she said equably, determined not to be put off by his cool manner. Turning to the boy she said, 'I have to go now, Ben, but before I do, here's a little something to play with.'

His eyes widened when she produced a small clockwork reproduction of the Eurocopter which she'd bought in the hospital shop.

'It's like the one that they brought me to hospital in!'

'Yes, it is,' she said softly, and with a quick glance at the man standing at the opposite of the bed she continued, 'And at this moment it's waiting for me up on the roof. Maybe when you're feeling better your daddy will let you have another ride in it as a special treat.' And on that suggestion she went.

CHAPTER FIVE

As KYLE watched Hannah go he groaned. Taking his eyes off his new toy for a moment, Ben asked, 'What's the matter, Daddy? Have you got a pain?'

Kyle shook his head. He hadn't got a pain. He was one! He was known to be cool, level-headed and unflappable, and yet whenever he was anywhere near Hannah he behaved like an idiot.

His heart had leapt when he'd seen her beside Ben's bed, and what had he done? Commented that she was on duty. A remark that she'd taken as a reprimand when it had been merely the first thing that had come into his head as he'd sought to conceal his pleasure.

Even if it had been meant in censure, he was well aware that the only time she would be able to get to see Ben would be during working hours. She was on duty until whenever the summer sun decided to set.

He also knew that she wouldn't have dreamt of coming onto the wards if there'd been the slightest chance she might be needed. And so what had he done? Antagonised her when she'd taken the trouble to visit Ben, instead of telling her how much he appreciated it, and how much her prompt action the day before had meant to him when his son had been so ill.

The temptation to go after her was strong, but it wasn't the right moment, was it? For one thing, he didn't want to upset Ben by dashing off. For another, Krasner and the paramedic would be up there, waiting for her, on the roof. He didn't want to be making his peace with her in front of them.

It would have to wait. He'd waited eight long years, so a couple of days weren't going to make much difference. His parents appeared at that moment, refreshed after their rest, and that was another reason for putting the talk to Hannah on hold.

'So what's wrong?' Jack asked Hannah as they flew back to base. 'Was the kiddiwink still poorly?'

'Er…no. Ben's doing fine,' she said absently.

'Then it's bad news about the bus-shelter woman?'

Hannah shook her head. 'No, not really. The news isn't good, but it isn't as bad as it could have been. I spoke to one of the A and E consultants before we left and he said that a skull X-ray had shown no internal bleeding but the leg fractures are very serious and it will be a long time before the lady can get about without assistance.'

'So what is it that's put your light out?' the pilot wanted to know. 'Templeton perhaps? You must have seen him when you went to visit the boy.'

She managed a smile. 'Don't be so nosy. I'm just tired, that's all.'

Not true, of course. A kind word from Kyle would have put her on cloud nine, but instead he'd had to remind her that she was on duty. Maybe he would have liked her to visit Ben in the middle of the night. The nursing staff would have loved that!

It transpired that late-night visiting *was* to be on the agenda but the other way round. Hannah had just got home when the doorbell rang and she found Kyle standing on the mat.

'I know you've only just got in so I'm not going to keep you,' he said, not meeting her surprised gaze. 'Ben is home and at this moment is tucked up in my bed. He's almost back to his usual self and I don't anticipate any more problems in that direction.'

'That's good,' she said quietly.

'Mum and Dad are in the spare room,' he went on, 'which makes us rather overcrowded and…er…I was wondering if you would consider having a lodger for the night?'

Into the stunned silence his request had brought about he said with an apologetic smile, 'I promise I don't snore.'

After his rebuff of the afternoon it was on the tip of her tongue to say, 'And what's wrong with your sofa?' But that would have been cutting off her nose to spite her face. To have Kyle so near for so long was a chance not to be missed, and so she said coolly, 'Yes, of course. But you'll have to give me time to make up the spare bed…and get out the red carpet.'

'Sure,' he agreed easily, ignoring the sarcasm. 'If I come down in an hour or so, will that be all right?'

'Yes, but you'd better take a key with you. I might have already gone to bed when you arrive.'

He was observing her blankly and she thought, That's taken the wind out of his sails.

She had no intention of being in bed on such an occasion, but it did no harm to let Kyle think that his presence was of so little importance that she just might be.

When she opened the door to him at just gone eleven o'clock Hannah saw him flinch and wondered why. She wasn't to know that her nightwear was the same as on the night that he'd stood in the shadows and watched Richard's departure, and that he was cursing inwardly because he was on the sidelines of her life and it was no one's fault but his own.

As she moved back to let him in, they brushed against each other and he became still.

But only momentarily. With a speed that left her speechless he reached out for her and pulled her to him.

'What is it with you, Hannah,' he breathed with his lips against the hollow of her throat, 'that you have us all wanting you? Krasner! The fellow you were seeing off so affectionately the other night and myself, just to name a few.'

She was listening to him openmouthed, her eyes bright blue pools of surprise beneath the ash blonde bob that was still damp from the shower.

It was difficult to know what to be the most amazed at—that Kyle had been watching when she'd sent Richard on his way and had obviously put two and two together and made five, or his admission that he was still attracted to her.

She pushed him away and as he stepped back she thought, This is crazy! I ought to be over the moon to know that he feels like that about me, yet I'm more concerned with putting him right about what's happening in my life.

But she had to explain the Richard business first. His comments regarding it had triggered off a degree of anger that would be a good antidote to any euphoria brought about by the discovery that he wasn't entirely immune to her presence.

'Where were you when I was saying goodbye to Richard?' she said coldly.

'Ah! So that was your friend Richard.'

'No! It was Richard who is an acquaintance of mine…and nothing more. He had called round to ask if I would like to go on holiday with him—'

'And he's only an acquaintance?' he questioned with a dry laugh.

'Yes! As I've already told you! But he's an acquaintance with an outsize ego and he couldn't believe it when I said no. Any affection you might have witnessed on my part was because I was feeling sorry for him in spite of his conceit. So now you know, and now *I* want to know how you came to be snooping on us.'

'Snooping!' he growled. 'I had just got out of the lift

and was about to call on you to discuss the arrangements for your minding Ben on the following day when I saw your door open, and before I could make my presence known you appeared with this fellow, Richard. And you have to admit that you weren't exactly overdressed.'

'As now?'

'Yes, Hannah, as now,' he confirmed with his voice deepening. There was an intensity in his dark gaze that was heating her blood. If he should take hold of her again she knew she would be lost.

She loved him, always had. Her feelings for him were like a pot that had once been on the boil and then been left to simmer for a long time, but now it was coming to the boil again, and she prayed that this time the right ingredients would be there.

'Have you any idea how beautiful you are, Hannah Morgan?' Kyle murmured.

She shrugged slender shoulders beneath the filmy robe and smiled across at him. 'You're quite spectacular yourself, Dr Templeton.'

This time she wasn't conscious of him taking her in his arms. All she knew was that she was there and it was where she wanted to be…always.

But as she gave herself up to the delight of the moment Hannah was only too aware that it was only minutes ago that she'd discovered how she affected him. Or maybe he'd talked that way because he was jealous of the other men who lusted after her?

If she and Kyle carried on like this, they would surely go on to make love. But when that happened she wanted it to be under different circumstances, with complete trust and peace between them. Not because she was dressed in flimsy night attire…and available.

Unaware that he was falling into a pit of his own making Kyle said softly, 'Shall we call a truce, Hannah?'

It would have been so easy to say yes but she couldn't let it go at that.

'Are you saying that you accept my version of what happened all that time ago with Paul as well?'

'I'm saying that I was a jealous fool who was too burnt up to stay and stake my claim.'

With a swift movement Hannah uncurled herself from his arms. 'But you're still not taking my version of events as the truth. You can't believe that my only interest in Paul was to offer comfort to someone at a time when they were weak and vulnerable!'

'Does it matter?' he asked bleakly as the magic began to disintegrate around him. The words he really wanted to say were sticking in his throat. It was just too painful to have to admit that his pride and stubbornness had been to blame for the wasted years.

'Yes, it does,' she cried. 'From where I am it looks as if I'm good enough to get sexy with, but not up to scratch in the honesty stakes. If you look in the cupboard over there you'll find a duvet and sheets for the spare bed. Goodnight, Kyle!' And turning her back on him, she stalked into her bedroom.

After a moment's silence he went to do as she suggested, with shoulders set and face shadowed in the light of the lamps.

So that was that, Hannah thought as she heard the spare room door close behind him with an angry click. She'd brought them both down from the clouds because she wasn't prepared to be patronised. To be accepted for one thing, but not another.

It was unbelievable that Kyle still had doubts about her, but it seemed that he had. How could he think that she would respond to him as she had and yet still be prepared to lie?

At just gone six o'clock the next morning she heard him

let himself quietly out of the flat, and when she looked in the spare room the bed linen was folded neatly on top of the mattress. If she hadn't known differently she would have said that the room hadn't been occupied.

So much for spending the night in his arms, she thought ruefully. She would be lucky if Kyle ever laid a finger on her again after the way she'd dismissed him in that hurtful moment of disillusionment.

As Hannah was leaving the apartment for another day's work it seemed as if the embarrassments of her relationship with Kyle Templeton were still presenting themselves.

When she reached the foyer they were all there—Kyle, Ben and his parents—waiting for the taxi that would take them to the station.

Her step faltered when she saw them, but Ben came running across and pushed a crumpled piece of paper into her hands.

'What's this?' she said gently as she knelt beside him.

'It's a ''thank you'' letter…for the helicopter. Daddy said he would give it to you, but now that you're here I'm giving it to you myself.'

She smiled. 'I see. Well, thank you, Ben. I'm so pleased to see that you're well again. Are you off to Grandma and Grandad's house now?'

He nodded. 'Daddy's coming to see us on Friday. Why don't you come with him, Hannah?'

She was conscious of Kyle hovering and if she hadn't been feeling so desolate the situation might have seemed amusing. His son inviting her to stay when she had just well and truly put the blight on their relationship…if it could be called that.

'Hannah has to work, you know, Ben. It wouldn't be easy for us both to be off at the same time,' he said stiffly, and then with the same tightness in his manner he went on,

'Let me introduce you to my parents. My mother, Grace Templeton, and my father, Howard,' he said. He turned to the older couple who were observing her with some surprise. 'Mum, Dad, meet Dr Hannah Morgan.'

'Delighted to meet you Dr Morgan,' Grace Templeton beamed. 'And our thanks for looking after our precious boy so well. It must have been very traumatic for you when he was taken ill so suddenly.'

Hannah smiled back at her. 'Just a bit.' She glanced at Kyle's sombre face. 'I know how much he means to you all, which isn't surprising. Ben is a delightful child.'

'He certainly is,' his grandfather agreed gruffly, and sent a quizzical look in his son's direction. 'The only thing he lacks is a mother.'

'Yes, well, if you'll excuse me I have to get moving,' she said quickly. 'The underground at this time of day is like the sardine special.' And with a quick kiss for Ben and another smile for his grandparents she was off.

'What a beautiful young woman,' Grace said when Hannah had gone. 'How long have you known her?'

Kyle's face was devoid of expression. What would she say if he were to tell her just how long? He wasn't going to, needless to say, but he could imagine the spate of questions that would follow if he did.

So he evaded the issue. 'Hannah is doing six months on the emergency unit before going into A and E consultancy.'

The big glass doors of the foyer opened at that moment to admit a taxi driver and he breathed a sigh of relief at being rescued from any further variations of the truth.

When the train had pulled out, with Ben waving vigorously through the window, Kyle walked towards the station exit with his shoulders hunched.

After last night's fiasco it had been an ordeal, seeing Hannah in the foyer of the apartments. He had done it again. Pride hadn't let him admit that he could have been wrong and now he was paying the price.

He loved the job, but today he had never felt less like presenting himself. But as he hailed a taxi his mouth softened. The helicopter emergency unit meant Hannah Morgan. She would be there as would he, and if they were once again at odds with each other, at least he could view her from afar.

The desire and tenderness she was arousing in him was spellbinding. But it would seem that after one step forward, they always took two steps back.

When he arrived at the unit all the medics were out, and as Kyle gazed around him in surprise the operations officer looked up from his control keyboard.

'There's been an explosion in a Chinese restaurant near Hammersmith Bridge and there are casualties.'

'How bad?' he asked.

'Serious,' the other man replied briefly. 'Smitty was on first call today and as soon as air traffic control had given us priority clearance they were off. The others followed by ambulance.'

Meeting Kyle and his family before she'd had a chance to get her mind round the happenings of the night before hadn't been the best start to Hannah's day. Not because she hadn't wanted to meet his parents or see Ben again. Both occurrences would normally have given her much pleasure. It was the man who'd stood by awkwardly as his son had innocently made matters worse by inviting her to visit them that had been the problem, and she was in no hurry to see him again.

For one thing, every time she saw him now there would be the memory of throwing away the chance to get closer to him because of her stupid pride. And of how Kyle hadn't been blameless either as he'd blighted the precious moment with his uncompromising remarks.

What was the matter with them both?

With regard to her brother-in-law, what else could she do to convince him, other than drag Paul here by the scruff of the neck and make him tell Kyle how she'd had no part in the big clinch he'd found them in?

Her smile was wry as she fought her way through the commuter crush. She could just see Paul's face if she did. Her ex-brother-in-law was lightweight in the extreme. He wouldn't have given a second thought to the time when he'd tried to use his dead wife's twin as a buffer to his misery, and had caused problems in her relationship with some other guy.

But in any case she wouldn't know how to find him. As she'd told Kyle, the last she'd heard of him he'd been living in the Midlands with a new wife.

It had been quiet for the first half hour of the day and then the call came through from the ambulance service centre. Explosion in a Chinese take-away. Serious injuries to staff and customers.

Smitty and his team were on their way in minutes and the rest of them followed by slower means to a scene of carnage.

'Looks like some kind of incendiary device,' the fire chief told them, 'but it's too early to say for certain. We've checked the premises and it appears to have been just the one. You can go in, but take care. There were a few minor fires but we've put them out.'

Hannah nodded and followed Pete inside. The place was still full of black smoke created by the blast, and as they groped their way past the counter, swaying drunkenly above a blackened carpet littered with glass, Hannah saw that there were still people inside.

The helicopter had been and gone and one of the ambulance crews who had called for the assistance of the fast response team told them, 'Your guy said he would come back once he'd seen the first casualty into A and E. The fellow was bleeding to death with an almost severed leg and the doctor was still trying to halt the blood loss as they took off.'

Pete was bending over an elderly Chinese woman and he said flatly, 'Life extinct. She must have taken the full force of the blast.'

'I've got a man here with head injuries and lacerations,' she told him urgently with a sombre glance at the old woman's still form. 'How long do you think Graham will be?'

'As long as it takes, I'm afraid,' he said grimly as he went over to where a teenage boy was sobbing uncontrollably with blood from a gaping cut running down his face.

'Shush, laddie. We're going to sort you out,' Pete told the youth gently as he stemmed the bleeding from the cut. He turned to the hovering paramedics. 'Take this young fellow to Casualty and we'll hang on for the chopper coming back. The other guy's head injuries will get seen to more quickly if we do it that way.'

'Where are we going to take him?' Hannah asked. 'King's?'

He nodded. 'Yes. King's or the Royal London. They're well organised for this kind of thing. But we'll see what Smitty says when he gets back.'

'What's the score here, then?' a familiar voice asked as she gave the injured man an injection to kill the pain. Hannah looked up to find Kyle there.

'One serious casualty has already been lifted off and we're waiting for the helicopter to come back for this one,' she said with cold brevity. 'We also have a fatality, and a teenage boy has just been taken to hospital with shock and cuts.'

If he felt the chill he didn't show it, but his face was grim as he informed her, 'The police say that they can't comment at this stage, but there's some sort of protection racket in this area and if the owner of this place wasn't prepared to pay up...'

Pete had joined them and he shook his head. 'Whatever the reason, I'll be glad to see the back of this place.'

Kyle nodded his agreement and with his dark gaze on Hannah said, 'I know that it's part and parcel of the job, but I'm not happy when any of you are in this kind of situation.'

It was on the tip of Hannah's tongue to tell him that she wasn't happy no matter what, but the noisy approach of the Eurocopter put paid to that, and perhaps it was just as well. Why should she humble herself by letting him see how much she cared, when all Kyle wanted was to use her when the mood took him?

When the second victim had been airlifted and an ambulance crew had taken the deceased woman to hospital for the official death certificate to be issued, Kyle said, 'I'll take Dr Morgan back with me, Pete.'

As the lanky medic eyed him questioningly he went on, 'Your wife rang just before I left base to say that she's developed some kind of bug since you left this morning and is feeling pretty rough. So I suggest that you take the rest of the day off.'

'Thanks. I will,' the other man said in quick concern. 'Is it all right if I use the car I came in instead of going back for my own jalopy?'

'Sure,' Kyle agreed easily. 'Be on your way. Our own are just as important when they're sick or injured as the rest of the population.'

Hannah sighed. She sympathised with Pete's problem entirely, but it meant that she would be in Kyle's company once again. Not in the sweet abandonment of the previous

night, but alone with him nevertheless, and at the moment
it was the last thing she wanted.

As she eased herself reluctantly into the seat beside Kyle
he said drily, 'I'm not going to bite, you know. If you move
any farther away from me you'll be falling out onto the
pavement.'

'Which might be preferable to sitting next to you,' she
snapped, irritated that he saw something to joke about in
her manner.

'I'm sorry,' he said levelly. 'I know that once again I've
upset you. It's as if there's a devil on my shoulder when
I'm with you. Maybe it's because you're such a disrupting
influence.'

'Huh! Not so disrupting that you ever tried to find me
during all the time we were apart,' she said tightly. 'I
searched for you everywhere. I even tried the hospital net-
work in America, as that was where we were both planning
to go for work experience. But you'd gone somewhere else,
hadn't you? Australia!'

'The reason I never came back until now was because I
did something very stupid during my first few months in
Queensland and it altered the course of my life. I became
a father to a child whose mother would have had him
adopted if I hadn't promised to bring him up myself. After
that I was no longer a free agent.'

'Did you love her?' Hannah asked painfully.

'I'm ashamed to say I didn't. She was a nurse at the
hospital who made a play for me.'

'And you let her?'

He sighed. 'Yes. I let her, and I didn't like myself for it
afterwards.'

So was she happy that Kyle hadn't loved this woman?
Hannah wondered. It didn't alter the fact that he'd sought
comfort elsewhere. But could she blame him for that, in
the light of what he'd seen as her betrayal?

'Was it the job with the helicopter medical service that brought you back…or something else?' she asked with a change of subject. 'Because whatever the reason you're still as proud and unbending as you were then!'

They were stopped at traffic lights and he gave her a quick sideways glance. 'Me proud and unbending! That's a good one. All I ever wanted in those days was the job and the girl. But one of them let me down and it wasn't the job.'

'Oh! For goodness' sake! Don't you like to play the role of the persecuted,' she hooted. 'The only thing I did wrong was to give Paul all the support I could. I realised afterwards that he'd been using me.'

Her voice thickened. 'And it was easy for him to do that because we were both grieving over the same person.'

'Which left me on the sidelines,' he said evenly, 'doing my damnedest to be supportive and understanding about a situation that seemed to be going on for ever.'

As she observed his grim profile Hannah thought, I can't believe this. Everything is coming out into the open. We're going to clear the air at last.

'And because you were so strung up about it you jumped to the wrong conclusions,' she told him. 'You obviously aren't aware of it, but Paul made it clear that he no longer needed a shoulder to cry on the moment he found a new love. I was left to pick up the pieces of my life, with you gone off in high dudgeon and my sister buried in a churchyard not far from where we lived. Some years before I'd coped with the death of first my mother and then shortly afterwards my father, and so I was well and truly alone, and if you think I'm begging for sympathy, Kyle, you're wrong.

'It's a strange thing about twins,' Hannah went on, with the fire gone out of her. 'So often they aren't seen as two separate beings, with their own hopes, dreams and feelings. Paul saw Janine and I as if we were one and expected me to take her place, which made it very hard to be supportive and yet keep him at arm's length.'

'And so that's how you're saying it was,' Kyle said flatly.

'Yes. I am.'

He sighed. 'So do I need to have a rethink?'

'You're the only person who knows the answer to that question,' she told him as he stopped the car on the fore-court way down below the operations room.

As they got out and faced each other across the bonnet Kyle said, as if the previous conversation had never taken place, 'I'm going home to see Ben at the weekend and I've promised him that I'll take you with me.'

Hannah's eyes widened. 'Wha-at?' she gasped. 'You might have asked me first!'

'If I'd done that you might have refused.'

'We can't both be off at the same time,' she protested weakly as the prospect of what he was suggesting took her breath away.

'I have a new doctor starting tomorrow,' he said blandly. 'He's had a lot of experience in A and E and will be my second in command. His name is Charles Conran. So you see, you can be spared.'

'Yes, I do see.'

'I don't think you do, but what about it, Hannah? You can't disappoint Ben.'

'All right. I'll come,' she agreed. 'As long as your parents don't mind. After all, it is their home.'

'It will be fine with them, I assure you.' And looking happier than he'd done all morning, Kyle shepherded her towards the lift that would take them upwards.

*   *   *

As the day wore on news of the morning's casualties came through. It appeared that the elderly Chinese woman had been the wife of the proprietor of the take-away. He had gone to the cash and carry at the time of the explosion and had been demented with grief on hearing what had happened to his wife.

The customer with the partly severed leg had been taken for microsurgery, and the man with head injuries had been diagnosed as having a fractured skull.

'All in all, not too cheerful,' Kyle remarked when the reports came in, 'but it could have been a lot worse without us.' As his glance rested on the only female member of his staff she was already wishing that she hadn't been so quick to accept his invitation for a weekend away.

She'd only met Kyle's parents once and Ben a couple of times, and her relationship with the boy's father was in such a delicate state that it needed nurturing rather than being sidetracked into 'happy families'.

But it was too late now. Both Ben and his dad would be hurt if she backed out. So at the end of a very strange day she prayed that she hadn't imagined a new closeness between Kyle and herself since they'd had that straight talk in the car.

CHAPTER SIX

ON THE Thursday morning Kyle asked Hannah, 'Which way would you rather travel on Saturday—by rail or road? I just haven't got around to getting myself a car since I came to London, but I can soon hire one.'

He went on to explain, 'One reason why I haven't bothered is because the tube is so handy, and for another it's more relaxing travelling to see Ben and my parents by train. Dad picks me up at the other end and if I need a car while I'm there he lets me use his.'

Hannah had smiled. She still couldn't believe that he'd invited her to spend the weekend with him. Even more amazing was this consideration for her wishes.

She was tempted to tell him that whatever kind of transport he laid on, it would be fine. That the back seat of a tandem or a slow-moving donkey would do just as well, as long as he and she were together.

But maybe she was being previous. She needed to remind herself that Kyle had asked her to join him because it was what Ben wanted.

Having seen him with the boy, she was aware that if his son asked for the moon he would try to lift it out of the sky for him. So thinking that Kyle was eager for her presence could be a mistake.

'The train will be fine,' she told him. 'No need to go to the trouble of hiring a car. Although I have to warn you that I shall probably sleep all the way.'

It was most unlikely, but a voice inside was warning her to keep him at a distance until his motives became clearer. In the last couple of days they'd made progress. They were

talking like reasonable people after the straight talk that
seemed to have finally cleared the air.

But, and there was always a 'but', the man she loved
could be unpredictable. Even though he appeared to have
accepted that he'd made a big mistake long ago.

With anyone else but Kyle she would have been walking
on air, but he had his own rules, his own standards, and
even though she knew he'd wanted to make love to her the
other night, it didn't mean that harmony was going to follow passion.

'Good,' he said, aware that her thoughts were wandering.
'I'll book a couple of tickets.'

'And what was all that about?' Jack asked as they flew
above the chimneypots minutes later in answer to a call for
assistance at a serious accident on a building site.

'What?' she parried innocently.

'You know! You and the boss being all chummy.'

Hannah laughed. 'We're going away for the weekend,'
she told him teasingly.

'What, you and Dr Templeton?' he joked back. 'I don't
believe it. What are you going to do? Chat about old
times?'

If he'd anything else to say he didn't get the chance. His
copilot, with map in hand, was pointing to a partly finished
office block, and on looking down they could see an ambulance and a cluster of workmen standing beside a still
figure on the ground.

Jack brought the helicopter down onto waste ground beside the building site, and as Hannah and the accompanying
paramedic raced towards the scene there was the familiar
chilling dread inside her as she braced herself for what she
was about to be faced with.

This time there were multiple injuries in keeping with a
fall from high scaffolding. The victim looked to be in his

late twenties, and though his hard hat had saved his head the rest of him was in a mess.

'My neck,' he was moaning as they reached him. 'I can't move my neck!'

'We're going to need temporary splints for his arms and legs,' she told the paramedic as she examined him. 'There are multiple fractures, and the neck rigidity indicates vertebrae damage, so we'll have to get him on to a spinal board before we can move him.'

'What happened?' she asked of a young police constable.

'Nobody knows. The fellow was up there on his own, so it wasn't a case of him being pushed.'

'Pushed! You're joking surely?' she cried.

He shrugged. 'It has been known.'

They'd been easing him onto the board while the police constable was propounding his theories and with a brief nod in his direction they moved off to where the pilots were patiently waiting to take on board their injured cargo.

That had been Thursday's major trauma, Hannah thought as she made her way home beneath the setting sun. The rest of the call-outs had been of a less serious nature, critical enough but not quite as bad as the poor fellow on the building site.

There had been no follow-up report on him so far, but when it did come through she wouldn't be surprised to hear that he'd been transferred to a spinal injuries unit.

Kyle had been still at his desk when she'd left and he'd beckoned her to go in as she'd passed the open door of his office.

'I won't keep you a moment,' he promised. 'Just tell me about this outing that's planned for tomorrow night at a restaurant in the Park Lane area. Graham Smith tells me that a table has been booked for a late-night meal for the

staff and anyone they wish to bring along. Are you going?'

Hannah shrugged. 'I don't know. I said I would when it
was first mentioned some weeks ago, but at that time I
didn't know I'd be travelling to Gloucestershire with you
the following morning. I'm presuming that you'll want us
to catch an early train so that you can spend as much time
as possible with Ben.'

'I think we should go,' he said. 'It's not fair to let the
others down. Added to that, this place isn't in the most
salubrious part of the city, so it's time we hit the high spots
for a change. Have you promised Krasner that you would
go with him? He always seems to be hovering when you're
around.'

'I wasn't intending going with anyone in particular. I
think Jack is bringing his current girlfriend. She's a receptionist at one of the Harley Street clinics.'

Kyle was smiling. 'Really? Jack the lad in more ways
than one, it would seem.'

'Mmm,' she agreed blandly. 'So, are we going or not?
And what train have you booked us on?'

'Yes. We're going. The train doesn't leave until mid-
morning…and if you oversleep it isn't far for me to come
and wake you up, is it?'

'Er…no,' Hannah agreed.

Nights were hot and airless in the capital in high summer
and the one that followed that particular discussion was no
different. In spite of having a fan in the bedroom and the
windows wide open, Hannah found herself unable to sleep
for the heat.

Her bedside clock said that it was half past two and,
throwing back the tangled sheets, she went into the kitchen
for a cold drink.

It was a moonlit night and as she looked down onto the

shadowed park below a longing came over her to be out there in the cooler night air.

There was no one about and no sooner had the idea come into her head than she was throwing off her short nightdress and reaching shorts and a halter top out of the wardrobe.

It *was* cooler in the park and very quiet. Seating herself on a nearby bench, she sat gazing up at the moon, but not for long. A taxi had just spilled out four revellers in a side road and, peering through the park railings, one of them saw her sitting there.

'Do you see what I see?' he said, and the others nodded amid noisy laughter.

Hannah had heard them and was on her feet. They sounded harmless enough, but at half past two in the morning she wasn't taking any chances.

The apartment block was only feet away, but to her dismay the men were lolling against the wall outside when she got there and when she took out her key one of them lurched towards her drunkenly.

She didn't get the chance to use it. The door swung open at that moment and Kyle reached out and pulled her inside.

'Stay there!' he ordered grimly, adding to the loiterers, 'I imagine that you have homes to go to. If you haven't moved on within the next five minutes I'm going to have to do something about it.'

'No need to get steamed up, buddy,' one of them said. 'We're going.'

'Are you insane, or what?' Kyle bellowed when they'd drifted off. 'Going out there at this time!'

'How did you know where I was?' she asked shakily.

He had been a most welcome sight as he'd flung the door open, but he'd been an unexpected one, too.

'You weren't the only one who couldn't sleep. I saw you

from my window, sitting on the bench as if it were the middle of the afternoon. Any inner city area is dangerous during these hours. You of all people should know that.'

'Will you please stop yelling at me?' she begged tearfully. 'I know it was a crazy thing to do, but I was so hot.'

He'd heard the tears in her voice and his face softened. 'How do you think I would feel if anything happened to you, Hannah?'

'I don't know. How would you feel?'

'I would feel guilty as hell.'

'But why? It wasn't you that put me at risk.'

He reached out and gently pushed her hair back off her damp brow. 'I would feel guilty because if our lives had run as they should have, you would have been in my bed tonight instead of wandering around a London park.'

'And that's it.'

'Yes, that's it, and now I'm going to see you to your door and will wait until you've locked it securely behind you.'

'Right,' she said limply. 'And, Kyle...'

'What?'

'Thanks for being there. I'm not used to it.'

'Huh? Not used to what?'

'Being looked after.'

As she lay once more in her solitary bed a short time later Hannah was smiling. Kyle hadn't laid a finger on her down there, except for dragging her quickly inside, but his concern for her had made her feel cherished and it was an unfamiliar but wonderful experience.

The next evening Hannah wore black again. The staff from the unit had all gone home to change once darkness had fallen and the Eurocopter had been put to bed, and when Kyle called for her she was only just ready.

Her dress was made of stiff silk, low cut with narrow

straps over the shoulders and a skirt that ended just above the knee.

It was a colour that complemented her hair and the pale smoothness of her skin, and with a choker of pearls and matching earrings she knew that she looked cool and elegant.

If she'd had any doubts about it his expression when he saw her would have put them to rest. Yet he merely remarked, 'You look good.' The degree of understatement told her he was on the defensive for some reason.

'So do you,' she replied in like manner.

Kyle was wearing a dark suit with a crisp white shirt and silk tie. Whatever her appearance was doing to him, his was making her feel weak at the knees.

He'd been attractive when she'd known him before, in a lean, restless sort of way, but time had calmed him down and taught him control, while at the same time filling him out physically.

A man in every sense of the word, he was strong, clever and darkly sensual…and added to that he was a loving father. It was the last thing she would have expected of the vibrant man that had been the Kyle Templeton of their youth, but she was looking at the mature version and he was something else.

'So? Are we ready?' he was asking. Bringing her mind back to more mundane things such as locking the door behind her and preceding him to the lift, Hannah answered the question in deeds rather than words.

'Whose idea was it to come here?' Kyle asked as they entered the muted elegance of the restaurant. Expensive leather furnishings and mellow wood panelling blended with quality tableware and linen, and beneath its soft lighting it was clear to see that this was an establishment to attract the discerning diner.

They were the first to arrive and as they settled down for

a pre-dinner drink Hannah looked around her. She was smiling and Kyle asked, 'What's the joke?'

'I'm just thinking about the staff of the helicopter emergency service dressed up to the nines in this place. It's a pleasant change from dashing out to try to save some poor soul…in our unbecoming surgical suits. And in answer to your question about whose idea was it to come here, the man himself has just arrived.'

Kyle looked around him. 'Who? Graham?'

'Yes. Apparently he used to come here with his wife before they had the children and he suggested it from a nostalgia point of view.'

'Well, it's certainly very classy. I hope none of our lot are looking forward to the Karaoke.'

It seemed that they weren't. They were all dressed for the occasion. Even Jack Krasner, whose clothes were invariably as casual as his manner, had made the effort.

The food and wines were excellent and expertly served. The company relaxed, and Hannah began to think she'd imagined Kyle being on the defensive as he faced her across the table.

She was seated next to Charles Conran, the latest member of the team and a widower for some years. The pleasant, balding newcomer had brought his sister with him and Hannah endeavoured to make them feel welcome on this their first foray into the social life of the unit.

But even so she was acutely aware of Kyle's eyes upon her all the time and there was something in his glance that she couldn't fathom.

What was going on in that mind of his? she wondered. They'd been close last night, or at least she'd thought they'd been, so surely it wasn't anything to do with her.

When they were ready to leave and the account had been presented in a beautiful leather folder, he reached across for it. As the rest of the party observed him in surprise, he

told them, 'Tonight is on me, folks. As a token of my
appreciation of the way you all give of your very best in a
job that's difficult, demanding and extremely nerve-
stretching.'

He raised his glass. 'A toast to the fastest medical response team in the city.' Amid good-natured laughter they
all followed suit.

Hannah was watching him thoughtfully. He had style. A
talent for taking the moment and turning it into something
special.

It was another warm night with a scattering of stars in
the heavens when they got outside, and Kyle said, 'How
about we walk part of the way before hailing a taxi? We'll
probably regret it in the morning when we have to make
an early start, but the night is too beautiful to just go home
and sleep.'

'Whatever you say,' she said dreamily. If he'd suggested
they throw themselves into the fountain in Trafalgar Square
she wouldn't have argued, so enchanted with the moment
was she.

As they walked slowly along pavements that had seen
many feet, Kyle took her hand in his. As his fingers tightened around hers, Hannah thought that to the casual ob-
server they would be taken for lovers strolling home to their
nest. So why not pretend that they were?

He stopped at last and turned to face her, his eyes shadowed in the light of the streetlamps.

'Have you ever thought about marriage?' he asked casually.

'What?' she gasped, not sure if she'd heard him cor-
rectly.

'I asked if you'd ever thought of getting married.'

'Yes, frequently,' she replied, rigid with amazement.
'Why do you ask?'

'I just wondered.'

'There has to be a reason why you would ask such a question.'

'I feel sometimes that I ought to provide Ben with a mother.'

Hannah's amazement was turning to anger. 'Am I missing something? Are you asking my opinion? Proposing to me? Or just making general conversation?'

'I'm proposing to you, Hannah. I can't let Ben go through life without the love of a caring mother.'

'I see.'

Did Kyle realise he was on a slippery slope? That glaciers were forming?

'Your son is adorable,' she told him with appropriate iciness, 'and I agree with your sentiments. But aren't you forgetting something? Being a mother is a very hard task when there isn't a loving husband to make up the trio. Unless my hearing isn't what it was, I haven't heard the word "love" mentioned with regard to you and I.

'You have some nerve, Kyle. What would the set-up be? Separate bedrooms? Or are you quite happy to take advantage of the chemistry between us? The old lust-without-love package? I knew that something was brewing the moment you called for me tonight, but I never expected it to be this.'

A taxi was cruising past and she hailed it, calling over her shoulder as she opened the door, 'Don't bother calling for me in the morning. I'm not going with you on the "happy families" weekend. I've lost the taste for it.'

Kyle hadn't spoken during her angry outburst. He'd just stood there like someone turned to stone. As the taxi moved off she looked through the back window and saw that he was still where she'd left him.

But he must have become mobile shortly afterwards, as

no sooner had she flung off the black dress and stripped off her underwear than he was ringing her bell.

When she didn't answer he went away, but within seconds the phone was ringing and it went on and on until, unable to stand the noise any longer, she picked up the receiver.

'You've had your say,' he said without preamble, 'and now, if I can get a word in edgeways, I have a comment to make. Not about us. That can wait. It's about the weekend. I shall be calling for you as arranged. Much as you and I aren't in tune at the moment, I know that you won't take it out on Ben. So be ready, Hannah.'

'And if I'm not?'

'I'll keep ringing the bell until you appear.'

'You have some arrogance!' she stormed.

He gave a dry laugh. 'Don't you believe it.' The line went dead.

When he'd replaced the receiver Kyle threw himself onto the bed and with his arms folded behind his head lay looking bleakly up at the ceiling.

Was he so self opinionated that he couldn't admit to being in the wrong? he thought raggedly. That he'd had to use Ben as an excuse for asking Hannah to marry him? It was small wonder she'd not been amused.

But he hadn't meant it to be like that. None of it had gone as planned. He'd intended waiting until they'd got back to her flat and then, after inviting himself in for a coffee, he would have told her how he felt and asked her to marry him.

But for some reason, out there in the magical starry night, he'd started to panic. Supposing she said no. Maybe she didn't love him. After all, he'd almost ruined both their lives. On the impulse of the moment he'd changed his tactics...with disastrous results.

He needed the coming weekend to put things right, if such a thing were possible. As he closed his eyes to the glare of the light above his head, he knew that if Hannah wasn't ready to do as he'd asked in the morning, he wouldn't know what to do next.

It was amazing. She had this effect on him. He was by nature quick-thinking and decisive, yet he'd asked the beautiful woman that she become Ben's stepmother, rather than his wife.

When he'd asked her she'd admitted that she thought about marriage frequently. Who to, though? There were other men in her life. Maybe it was one of them that she languished over.

For God's sake! Where was his confidence? It wasn't usually in short supply, but of late he wasn't thinking straight when it came to his private life.

When Hannah opened the door to Kyle next morning, dressed in a linen suit the colour of her eyes and holding a weekend case, he felt relief wash over him.

She was coming, thank goodness! He hadn't entirely put the blight on their relationship. But her expression wasn't exactly reassuring. The frost warning was still in place and there were no signs of a thaw as they took their seats on the train.

When it was announced that the buffet car was open Kyle got to his feet. 'I'm going to search out some breakfast. I didn't have time to eat before we left. Can I get you anything, Hannah?'

He wasn't going to tell her that he hadn't slept until dawn was breaking and then, having finally dozed off, he'd been woken up by the alarm.

There was irony in her bright blue gaze and he flinched. Hannah saw it and knew he understood that what she wanted of him was more than he seemed prepared to give. Not a bacon butty or soggy toast, but respect, and if he was capable of it…love.

'A cup of tea would be fine,' she said smoothly, and as she watched his broad back moving in the direction of the buffet car her doubts about the weekend ahead returned.

It was lunacy to be allowing herself to be manoeuvred into the bosom of his family. What purpose could it serve? Maybe Kyle thought she would weaken when she was with Ben, but if he did he was mistaken.

The small, fair-haired boy would be hard to resist. But just suppose she did agree to his father's proposal, what about Kyle's parents? What would they think of Ben being landed with a mother that he hardly knew?

At last, after what seemed like a lifetime of meaningful silences, the train pulled into the mediocre station that didn't do justice to the beautiful town of Cheltenham Spa.

Howard Templeton was waiting for them on the platform, with Ben clinging to his hand, and as she watched Kyle's face light up Hannah thought that he couldn't be blamed for wanting the best for his son.

But he had a strange way of going about it. Kyle should be aware that if any stepmother that he found for his son wasn't happy, it would wash off onto Ben.

What was the matter with the man? Why couldn't he organise his private life as well as he ran the unit? There wasn't a person there who didn't admire his intelligence and organisational skills.

As she watched Kyle swoop Ben up into his arms the boy smiled at her over his shoulder and she smiled back, suddenly glad that she'd come.

'Guess what, Hannah?' he said as they made their way to the car.

'What?'

'Grandma is making me a doctor's suit like yours and daddy's.'

'Really?' she exclaimed, suitably impressed.

When she looked up Kyle was smiling across at her, and if she'd been sure that it wasn't because he was sizing her up for the job, she might have felt like smiling back.

His parent's house, beside a clear stream, was built from the same golden Cotswold stone as all the other buildings in the village, and to Hannah, whose residences for a long time had been of the flat or apartment variety, it was enchanting.

Kyle was watching her expression. 'So what do you think?' he asked.

'Lovely!'

'Would you like a house like it?'

'Mmm.'

Then as the thought came to mind that it might be the bonus that went with the job of stepmother, she added, 'But I'm quite happy where I am.'

His face sobered. He'd got the message, she thought, and if he didn't like it...

As they went inside his mother came out of the kitchen, her face flushed from the heat of the stove.

'How lovely to see you, my dear,' Grace Templeton said. 'I'm sure you must be weary after the journey. If you'd like to freshen up Kyle will show you to your room.'

When they reached the upstairs landing and were out of earshot, he said grittily, 'You don't have to worry about my parents. They haven't invited you here to look you over as prospective wife material. My mother is under the impression that I haven't known you long.'

'Why did you tell her that?' Hannah asked coldly.

'Because she knows that I had an unfortunate experience a long time ago that affected my views on the opposite sex, and I didn't want her to know that you were involved.'

'How kind of you to protect my reputation!' she snarled. 'Except that there's no need.'

If Kyle had anything to say to that he didn't get the chance as Ben was leaping up the stairs towards them to say that they would be eating in ten minutes.

Hannah's room was at the front of the house, next to where Kyle would be sleeping with Ben, and as she looked out across cornfields to the hills beyond, the hustle and bustle of London seemed far, far away.

'So how are you liking life on the helicopter unit?' Grace asked as Hannah helped her clear away after the meal.

'It's very different,' she said politely. 'I've worked in accident and emergency for a long time, and usually it's the casualties that are brought to us, whereas on the fast response unit we go out to them. It's horrific sometimes what we have to deal with, but the results are fantastic. The badly injured are lifted into care so much faster that lives are saved where they might have been lost.'

'Yes. I can see that,' her hostess said, 'and once your six months is up, what will you do then?'

Good question, Hannah thought, and wondered what Kyle's mother would say if she were to tell her that until a short time ago she'd had her life planned. But after meeting up with her son again she could no longer see the way ahead clearly.

'Kyle tells me that you haven't known each other long,' Grace went on, 'which I suppose is understandable if you're only in training for six months.'

At that moment Hannah had a sudden overwhelming urge for the truth to be brought out into the open.

'I'm aware that's what he told you, but the truth is we've known each other a long time, Mrs Templeton,' she said levelly, 'and have recently met up again.'

With her hands covered in suds from the sink his mother turned slowly. 'Were you the one who broke his heart?' she asked quietly.

Hannah sighed. She'd wanted the truth out in the open, but it wasn't that easy when it came to explanations.

'Not intentionally, I can assure you,' she said quietly. 'I'd lost my twin sister in a car accident, which left her husband inconsolable. As could be expected, he turned to me for support. I looked like her, thought like her, and the rest.

'Paul had always been a bit neurotic and I gave him moral support for months. He wanted me there all the time, and where at first Kyle understood and kept a low profile he began to be weary of me never being there for him. We were deeply in love and although I sensed he wasn't happy it never occurred to me that he might think I'd transferred my affections to Paul.

'Kyle came in one day and caught me in his arms and it was the last straw. I tried to tell him that it had been Paul overreacting again. That he was supposed to have been giving me a peck on the cheek, but it had turned into a full-scale embrace that I couldn't fight my way out of.

'Your son was living in hospital accommodation at the time and when I went to his flat the next day he'd gone. I never saw him again until a few weeks ago when he came to take over the unit.'

His mother was leaning limply against the sink, the soapy water from her hands making a small pool on the floor.

'And how does he feel about you now, Hannah?' she croaked.

'I wish I knew. I feel that he still has reservations about me and always will have.'

'I know that he was bitterly hurt at the time,' Grace said, 'but Kyle always kept his affairs to himself and we never got to know much about what had happened. It seems as if it put him off marriage, but didn't stop him from taking on the role of fatherhood. What do you think about him bringing Ben up on his own?'

'I think he's to be greatly admired. Not many men would do a thing like that.'

'No, they wouldn't. I'm proud of my son, Hannah,' Grace said, 'but he can be very stubborn at times.'

'I do know that!' Hannah agreed, and the two women laughed.

'There has to be a reason why neither of you have married,' his mother went on, turning back to the sink, 'and needless to say I shall keep my fingers crossed. I won't breathe a word to Kyle about our little chat.'

As she went to find the others Hannah wondered what Grace would think if she knew about his proposal of the previous night. But that was something she was going to keep to herself and she hoped he was going to do the same.

'That was a long chat you were having with my mother,' Kyle said as they played with Ben in the last few minutes before his bedtime.

'Hmm, wasn't it?'

'Are you going to tell me what it was about?'

'No.'

'So I'm still out of favour, am I?'

'Yes. Even more so now I've discovered that you're sparing with the truth.'

'I'm not with you.'

'Telling your mother that we've only just met.'

'I've explained why I did that and, also, if I'd told her the truth, Mum would have started asking questions and I can do without that.'

'Hard lines. Because as *I've* nothing to hide, I've told her about the past. Although she immediately guessed who I was when I told her we'd known each other a long time ago. She asked if I was the one who broke your heart.'

He tutted angrily. 'And what did you say?'

'I just told her the truth. That the heartbreak you suffered was self-inflicted.'

Hannah watched his face whiten, whether with pain or anger she wasn't sure, but she immediately felt guilty. What she'd just said wasn't strictly true.

She knew that she hadn't been fair to him during the months after her sister's death. He'd been kind and considerate for many long weeks while she'd been at Paul's beck and call, and she should have had the sense to have seen that he wouldn't put up with it for ever. That they'd been entitled to a life of their own.

In the months that had followed Kyle's angry departure Paul had shown no concern for her anguish as she'd searched frantically for him, and she'd come to the conclusion that her brother-in-law was a selfish manipulator.

'I'm sorry for saying that, Kyle,' she said, reaching out to him. 'I may not have been guilty of what you thought, but I wasn't blameless. I put Paul before you and our life together, and I shouldn't have done. If I have an excuse it's that I wasn't thinking straight at the time.'

Ben was tugging at her skirt, and as she looked down at him he cried, 'I've lost the ball in the bushes, Hannah.'

'Then let's go and look for it, shall we?' she said, allowing the tensions of the moment to dissolve as the problem of a lost ball took priority.

CHAPTER SEVEN

WHEN Ben had gone to sleep Hannah and Kyle sat in the garden with his parents. While Howard regaled his son with tales of village happenings, Grace gently probed into Hannah's background.

When she heard that Hannah was alone in the world, that both her parents and her sister were dead, the older woman said gently, 'Life hasn't been very kind to you in lots of ways, has it, my dear? Those of us whose families are intact take it for granted, I'm afraid, which makes us seem rather selfish.'

Hannah was conscious that Kyle was tuning in to what they were saying, even though he was giving a good pretence of listening to his father.

'You must get Kyle to bring you again,' his mother went on. 'It's clear that Ben likes having you here, and that old love of mine has been perkier than I've seen him in ages, having a beautiful young woman around the place.'

Hannah's smile was wry. 'Which only leaves Kyle.'

'Give him time,' Grace suggested. 'I'm sure that bringing you here today wasn't just for Ben's benefit.'

Kyle was getting to his feet and Hannah knew immediately that he was going to break up their chat.

'Can I get anyone a drink?' he asked.

Both his parents shook their heads and his father said quizzically, 'Your mother and I will be having our bedtime cocoa soon. We love having Ben with us, but we're not as young as we used to be and once he's asleep we aren't far behind. That way we're ready for him when he awakes at crack of dawn.'

Kyle had a worried frown on his face and Hannah thought that maybe having Ben was too much for his mother and father. Perhaps that was why he'd done her the honour of proposing.

By half past nine they were alone in the summer gloaming and Hannah felt her nerve ends tighten. They'd been given this chance to talk and suddenly she couldn't face it.

She got to her feet. 'I think I'll have an early night, too.'

Kyle didn't move out of his chair, but as she walked past him he reached out and gripped her wrist. 'Not so fast, Hannah,' he said softly. 'What's the rush?'

Having been stopped in her tracks, she looked down at him. 'There's no rush. I'm just tired, that's all.'

He was on his feet now, still preventing her from moving on and as they faced each other, in defiance on her part and with a calm authority on his, Hannah knew that it was a moment when reason was going to be in short supply, and desire the ruling force.

Their responses to each other at times like this were faster than any force on earth, with Kyle tall, dark and demanding and herself melting in the fire that was sparking between them.

He'd released her wrist and was cupping her face in his hands. There was a hunger in his eyes that matched her own and in that second it was all that mattered. The fact that they never got anything else right was forgotten.

A summer moon looked down on them benignly as they came together, mouth to mouth, breast to breast, thigh to thigh, with the only thing stopping them from making love on the cool green grass of the lawn the fact that Kyle's parents were preparing for bed in a room overlooking the garden.

It was perhaps as well, Hannah thought as they drew apart at last. It was preventing her from making a fool of herself. She'd come away against her will because of a promise to a small boy. He'd been used as an inducement behind a hurtful marriage proposal, and so far nothing had changed.

The fact that she'd turned Kyle down flat might have something to do with her not having been invited to share Ben's bedtime story. She'd heard his father's deep voice reading to him in the next room and gradually it had gone quieter, until at last it had stopped and she'd known that the boy had fallen asleep.

To be left out was only a small thing but it had hurt, and when they'd come face to face on the landing she'd told Kyle that she would have liked to have been part of the nightly ritual.

He'd given her a dry smile and had told her, 'No point in letting Ben get too close to you. He'll only be upset when you go.'

She'd stared at him stonily. 'Go?'

'Yes. Out of our lives. Don't forget, you won't be with the unit for ever, and I don't want to pick up the pieces.'

'All this is because I refused to take on the role of his stepmother, isn't it?' she'd cried. 'If you aren't the most insensitive man I've ever met, I don't know who is!'

And now here she was. Heart thumping, legs like jelly, the age old longing bringing her blood to fever heat. Yet knowing that as things stood there was no future in it.

'So? Is it all right if I go to bed now?' she asked weakly.

'You mean now that we've established that we agree on one thing at least…and don't pretend that you don't know what I mean, Hannah. It's better now than it ever was.'

As her colour rose in a warm tide Hannah was glad of the darkness. She couldn't deny what he'd said. The second they touched the magic was there. What a pity it wasn't the same when it came to words.

'If you think so,' she said casually, and without a backward glance went into the house.

* * *

If there had been stresses the night before they weren't in evidence the next morning when Hannah went downstairs to find Grace at the stove, her husband engrossed in the Sunday papers and Kyle supervising Ben's breakfast. It was a tranquil domestic scene and she felt like an intruder.

'Hi, there,' Kyle said easily as she stood framed in the doorway.

Ben waved a milky spoon in her direction.

'We're going to take you out to lunch, Hannah,' the little boy said as the last of his cereal disappeared.

Kyle laughed as he ruffled his son's fair crop. 'You're a bit ahead of us, young man. Hannah hasn't had her breakfast yet.'

Pushing away her moment of depression, she smiled back. 'That will be lovely, Ben.'

'I thought that it would give you the opportunity to see something of the countryside,' Kyle explained, 'or the town if you prefer it, leaving Mum and Dad to have a quiet day.'

She nodded, remembering his concerned expression of the night before.

'I'd like to explore Cheltenham if that's all right with you,' she told him. 'I've heard that it's a beautiful town.'

'It is indeed,' his mother agreed. 'A tasteful mingling of the old and the new.'

'Then the shops and the Promenade it is. Ben and I will take you on a guided tour,' Kyle promised, 'but first you must eat.'

The Promenade was one of the most beautiful parts of the famous spa town, with the Queens Hotel, fronted by flower-filled public gardens, at the one end and the city centre at the other. An imposing thoroughfare, it was made up of smart shops on the one side and imposing terraces of Regency houses and offices on the other.

They'd strolled through Montpelier, another elegant area

with artistic overtones, and now, with Ben trotting along between them, they were on the Promenade.

An elderly lady passed them, serenely riding a bicycle that would have graced a museum, and Hannah and Kyle exchanged amused glances.

There was a graciousness about the place that spoke of past wealth, beautiful buildings built in the days when the rich had come to take the waters, and everywhere there were flowers.

'So, which would you prefer?' he asked. 'An elegant Regency town house, or somewhere like Mum and Dad's place?'

Was he putting out feelers again? she wondered. Kyle knew perfectly well that the grand terraces all around them weren't the right sort of place to bring up a child. Ben was in the best possible place where he was, in a quiet Cotswold village.

'Why do you keep asking me what kind of house I would like?' she asked casually. 'The decision isn't likely to arise. I've always travelled light. I don't put down roots.'

Their eyes met above Ben's head.

'Am I to blame for that?' he asked.

'Partly, but we've gone over all that, Kyle. I thought we'd agreed that we were both at fault.'

He nodded. 'Yes. I suppose so. But we do have to talk, Hannah.'

'We can do that on the train this evening,' she suggested, still with the reluctance to discuss anything other than generalities.

She had an awful feeling that the sheer force of her love for him might make her agree to his proposal and if she did that she would be a crazy woman.

Kyle might be even more keen for her to marry him, having heard what his father had said the night before. So if he brought it up again she could be sure that he felt he had another reason to push the suggestion. Any reason but the right one.

'Would you like to have lunch at the Queens Hotel?' he asked with a change of subject.

She smiled. 'Yes and no.'

'Meaning?'

'That where you and I might find it to be the right place for us, I'm sure that it isn't suitable for a lively seven-year-old. I suggest we let Ben decide.'

He groaned dramatically, 'And we both know where that will be, don't we?'

'I want my lunch at—' Ben began.

'McDonald's!' they chorused laughingly.

And when he asked, 'How did you guess?' they laughed even more.

They hadn't been back at Kyle's parents' house long when the doorbell rang. When Howard came back after answering it he said in a surprised tone, 'It's someone for you, Hannah.'

She was just about to shake the dice in a game she was playing with Kyle and Ben, but her hand remained suspended in mid-air as she took in what he was saying.

'For me?' she echoed, without moving out of her seat.

Kyle's expression was as surprised as hers. 'Hadn't you better go and see who it is?' he suggested.

Hannah jumped to her feet. 'Yes, of course.'

She was smiling as she went into the hall. It was obviously a mistake of some kind. She didn't know a soul in the area.

When she saw the man waiting there the smile was wiped off her face and her legs turned to jelly.

'So it *is* you!' Paul cried.

He moved across and took her into his arms and as she stood stiffly in his embrace he went on, 'I saw you getting into a car in the town centre and thought I was seeing things. I followed it and here I am. How are you, Hannah? And what are you doing here?'

Before she could reply a movement behind them had him looking up, and with his talent for creating awkward situations he cried, 'I *thought* it was Templeton you were with.'

His glance went to Ben, who was standing beside his father. 'So you two did get married after all?'

'I'm afraid not,' she said limply as the past rose again like a tormenting spectre. 'Ben is Kyle's son...and I'm just visiting.'

She was extricating herself from Paul's arms with her eyes on Kyle's face, and the look on it wasn't reassuring.

'So you live in these parts, do you?' he asked of Paul with cold politeness.

'Yes. I have a house in Charlton Kings.'

Paul turned to Hannah again as if she was the only one that mattered. 'I told you the last time we met that I'd married my secretary, didn't I? Well, now I've got two daughters.'

'That's nice for you,' she said flatly, resisting the urge to tell him that she might have had a family of her own by now if it hadn't been for him.

Grace was hovering. 'Would your friend like to join us for dinner, Hannah?'

She could feel herself cringing. If he said yes she would want to disappear. But for once the fates were kind.

'I can't, thanks just the same,' he said disappointedly. 'My wife has invited some friends round and she'll be expecting me. But I'll be free tomorrow. We could meet up somewhere, Hannah.'

'I'm afraid that I'm going back to London tonight,' she said quickly.

Paul was frowning and from past experience she knew he didn't like to be thwarted. 'Can't you stay on a day?'

She almost felt like laughing. Kyle's expression would be worth seeing if she said she would, especially to please Paul of all people!

'I can't. For one thing Kyle is my boss and he wouldn't agree as we have a very demanding job, and for another it's so long since we last met I can't think of anything we could have to say to each other.'

Hannah opened the front door. It was an ungracious thing to do, but she couldn't wait to see the back of him and for once he took the hint.

'You knew he lived in Cheltenham, didn't you?' Kyle said darkly as they went back to join the others.

'Of course I didn't!' she snapped back angrily. 'You heard what he said. He spotted me in the town centre. If I'd wanted to see Paul again I would hardly have asked him to come here, would I?'

'One would think not, but I don't know what's going on in your mind, do I?' he said wearily. 'But once a limpet always a limpet. You won't have seen the last of him.'

'Really? And how do you make that out? Did you hear me give Paul my address or phone number?'

The meal was on the table and it was time to eat instead of arguing. For that she was suitably grateful.

The train back to London was at seven o'clock and Ben was allowed to stay up to see them off at the station. There were no tears, and as it pulled out Kyle said sombrely, 'The fact that Ben can say goodbye so easily is a relief to me. It shows that he's totally happy with Mum and Dad. But from their point of view I'm not so sure that I'm being fair to them. You heard what Dad said?'

'Yes, I did,' she said levelly. 'But I don't think he meant you to take it that they couldn't cope. It's just the generation gap. See how things work out, but keep your eye on them nevertheless… And if I were you I would start doing some serious house hunting.'

He nodded. 'Thank you for the words of wisdom. And now tell me, have you enjoyed the weekend that you were so doubtful about...with its unexpected bonus?'

'Bonus?'

'Yes. The visit from your brother-in-law.'

'Now you're being ridiculous. Do you honestly think I wanted to see Paul? I owe him nothing. If I'd known he was around I'd have been even more doubtful about coming to Cheltenham. But in the first instance *you* were the initial cause of my reluctance.'

Here we go! Kyle thought. Hannah was presenting him with the opportunity she'd avoided all the time they'd been away—a chance to discuss the other unsettled half of his life. Maybe for once he would say the right thing.

'I'm sorry that I upset you by asking you to marry me,' he told her flatly. 'It must have been the magic of the night that made me feel that all our problems were so easily solvable. I said it on impulse and immediately regretted it.'

'So you didn't mean it?' she asked incredulously as outrage rekindled.

He'd meant it all right, he thought, but not in the way it had come over. And now, if he started to explain, would she believe him?

'Why don't we put all our differences behind us, Hannah, and start afresh?' he said quietly, but he saw that it wasn't going to be that easy.

'And just supposing I'd decided to accept your proposal. What then?' she asked coldly. 'I might have thought I'd take what was on offer because Ben is so lovable. I would look a fool now, wouldn't I, seeing that you didn't mean it? I don't understand you, Kyle. I don't think I ever will, but there's one thing I do know...'

'And what's that?'

'You have the power to put the blight on my life more

than anyone I've ever met.' She pulled a magazine out of her bag, 'And now if you'll excuse me…'

For the rest of the journey Hannah pretended to read, with Kyle sitting beside her in grim silence. When they arrived at the other end she would have given the earth for them to have lived at opposite ends of the city instead of on each other's doorstep, but she needn't have worried.

'I'm calling in at the helipad to make sure that all is in order for tomorrow,' he said tonelessly. 'Krasner is on holiday for two weeks and I want to check that his replacement is geared up and ready for action. Goodnight, Hannah.'

'Goodnight,' she replied stiffly, and left him to watch her departure with bleak resignation.

Monday morning was chaotic and Hannah was thankful for it.

The helicopter was required the moment it arrived on site and as it was her turn to be on first call there was no time for any exchange of words with Kyle other than a brief greeting.

A call had come through from Ambulance Emergency Centre to say that there'd been a derailment and that all available vehicles and personnel were needed.

In view of the seriousness of the incident Kyle told Pete Stubbs to go with her and as the Eurocopter took off the rest of the unit were hurrying to ground level where the cars were parked.

The relief pilot was a surly individual who knew the job and that was all, whereas the absent Jack, whose skills never ceased to amaze Hannah, had the ability to make even the most dangerous mission seem fun.

As if Pete had read her mind, he said in a low voice, 'Come back, Jacko. We need you.'

It was bad. Very bad. An empty goods train had collided with a packed commuter train between stations and the front carriages of both were telescoped grotesquely across the tracks.

A stream of ambulances was arriving and police cars were dotted about the scene. As they surveyed the carnage below Pete muttered, 'This is not good. Not good at all. There are going to be fatalities if I'm not mistaken and probably some horrific injuries.'

'Let's get to them, then,' Hannah said with her heart thumping. The moment the chopper landed she was out, with Pete right behind her.

'Are we glad to see you,' a police officer said as they approached.

Beside him people were lying on the embankment or staggering around in shock, with ambulance crews trying to sort out the injured from those who were just traumatised.

'What's the score?' Hannah asked briefly.

'There are folk trapped in the derailed carriage of the commuter train.'

'And the other?'

He shook his head.

'There was just the driver on board. When we pulled him out he was dead.'

As they ran to the mangled mess of the first carriage he called, 'We're waiting for the fire brigade. There's a lot of fuel about.'

'So?' Pete said with a wry smile. 'As long as nobody lights a match...'

It was dark inside and there was twisted metal everywhere, with a haze of black dust hanging over it.

Two paramedics were bending over a screaming woman who was trapped by her legs, and Hannah could see the arm of a child sticking out from beneath a pile of mangled upholstery. A dark-haired man in a suit was lying unconscious across what was left of a table. And that was just for starters. What was going on in the rest of the carriage they couldn't stop to find out.

Pete had gone to help the paramedics free the trapped woman and Hannah was flinging the debris off the child, frantic to see if he was still alive.

She could feel tears running down her cheeks. Suppose it had been Ben, she thought illogically.

'I'll see to this,' Kyle's voice said suddenly at her side. 'You have a look at the guy in the suit.'

Speechless with relief, she ran across to him and as she did so there were flashes of yellow in the gloom of the carriage and men's voices calling to each other. The fire brigade had arrived.

The man lying motionless over the table had severe chest injuries. The front of his shirt had been ripped open and she could see deep lacerations as if he had been flung forward with such force that his chest had taken the brunt of the impact. His neck was at an odd angle, too, but he was alive. There was a heartbeat and a strong pulse, but against that they had to get him out without injuring him further.

The firemen were moving down the carriage, followed by reinforcements from the ambulance service, and two of them had stopped to help Kyle get to the child.

They must have managed it because she heard him cry, 'Don't move him until I've examined him. Bring a stretcher!'

'Bring two!' she cried. 'This man is going to need one.'

One of the paramedics from the unit had appeared by her side and as they put a collar on the injured man he said nervously, 'They've managed to get the people out from the other end of the carriage. We're the only ones still inside and there's a big fire risk from leaking diesel.'

'I can't help that,' Hannah told him. 'We have three patients here who can't be left. Pete is treating the woman they've just freed. Kyle is with the child and he won't let him be moved until he's sure that it's safe to do so.'

The paramedic looked around him. 'Yes, but it's not safe, is it? This place could go up like a tinder box any minute.'

Ignoring his panic, she went on, 'And this poor man will be someone's much-loved son, husband or father…and we can't leave him.'

Eventually they were out…all of them…the injured and those treating them. Hannah breathed a sigh of relief. The paramedic's forebodings had affected her, in spite of trying to ignore them, but the danger was over.

Fortunately, the boy who'd been trapped had been the least hurt of the three, so he had been taken away by ambulance. The man in the suit had been flown to the Royal London after she had phoned with full details of his condition, and the woman, who had serious leg injuries, was waiting for the helicopter to come back for her.

As fast as Hannah was telling herself that the danger was over it became apparent that maybe it wasn't. At that moment a woman who'd been lying on the grass in a shocked state sat up and cried, 'My mother! Where's my mother?'

There was no reply and Hannah and Kyle looked at each other. If the mother wasn't here on the embankment she must still be in the train. Unless she'd been taken to hospital.

'Where were you sitting?' a policeman asked.

'At the back of the first coach,' she screamed. 'She'd gone to the toilet.'

There were firemen still on board, dousing the wreckage to prevent fire, but they hadn't yet reached the part the woman had described.

When they heard that someone was missing they stopped and converged on the flattened toilet area, and to the horror of all those on the embankment came the cry, 'She's here! Send the doc on board.'

There were only the two of them, Kyle and herself. Graham had gone in one of the ambulances with a badly injured victim and Pete and Charles had gone with the helicopter.

Instinctively Hannah stepped forward, but a firm hand pulled her back.

'I'm taking this one,' Kyle said. 'It's too risky for you.'

As she opened her mouth to protest he went on, 'I'm in charge, don't forget.' And with a dry smile he was gone.

After that each second was an eternity and when someone on the embankment cried, 'It's on fire!' Hannah went cold with horror.

Sure enough, flames were licking around the toilet area, and she thought desperately that if Kyle came out of this alive she would marry him on any terms, just as long as she could be with him.

A smouldering cigarette end dropped in the carriage had started the blaze, but it hadn't reached the leaking fuel and as the rest of the fire brigade converged upon the flames a sigh of relief went up from those on the bank as the injured woman was carried out followed by Kyle and the firemen.

He was bending over her and Hannah ran across to assist him with tears spilling down her cheeks. Looking up briefly he said, 'Surely those aren't for me?'

'What?' she croaked.

'The tears.'

'Of course they are. I thought you were going to die.'

The woman they had just rescued was unconscious, but apart from cuts and bruises she seemed to have had a remarkable escape. Clearly there might be other injuries not immediately obvious, but as Kyle cut away her clothing to check that they hadn't missed anything it seemed as if she had been incredibly lucky.

Her daughter was weeping quietly beside her and Hannah thought that what had probably been the start of a pleasant day's shopping had turned into a nightmare.

When all the casualties had been taken to hospital and the police and fire brigade had given the all-clear, they drove back to the unit.

Hannah still in a chastened state of mind and Kyle irritatingly whimsical about what could have been the most devastating day of her life.

'I made a vow while you were inside the train,' she told him after a long silence on her part.

'Really? What was it?' he asked casually.

'That if you asked me again I would marry you on any terms.'

If she'd wanted to take the wind out of his sails she couldn't have thought of a better way. He almost ran into the car in front in his amazement and without more ado he pulled to the side of the road.

'Would you like to repeat that?'

'You heard me the first time,' she said quietly.

'Mmm. I admit that I did. I just wanted to hear you say it again.' As Hannah sat immobile, awaiting his response, she felt that in the next few moments her life could be changed for ever.

She was presuming too much. He was about to put her crazy admission into perspective.

'Thanks a bunch for offering yourself up as the sacrificial lamb,' he said coolly, 'but just as you didn't like my approach when I mentioned marriage, I'm not over the moon at yours.

'Was it perhaps that you were concerned about what would happen to Ben if I died? Or maybe you were overwrought after the trauma of the derailment.'

It was the obvious moment to tell him that if anything had happened to him she would have wanted to die, too.

That she loved him desperately, and that any sort of relationship was better than none. But would he believe her? He'd already turned her offer into a joke.

'It's quite clear that you doubt my sincerity,' she told him wearily, 'so let's forget it, shall we? I wish I'd never got involved with you again, Kyle. You're a disruptive presence in my life which I can do without, and if you don't want them sending out a search party for us I suggest we get back to the unit.'

Kyle's state of amazement continued throughout the day. Hannah had offered to marry him whatever the circumstances, and where he would have expected to have been delighted, he was anything but.

It was significant that where there had been no mention of love in his offer of marriage, the same applied to hers. What was the matter with them both?

Passion kindled between them faster than the speed of light, but what about the basics of a good marriage? Love? Trust? Honesty?

She was beautiful and kind and no way was he going to let her get involved in a marriage of convenience. He'd made a nice mess of things and it seemed that for the present he was going to have to let her get on with her life.

'Disruptive' was how she'd described him and it hadn't been meant as a compliment.

As doctor on call Hannah was out again within minutes of their return, and for the rest of the day they made a point of avoiding each other.

The reports had come through on the casualties from the derailment. The child had been kept in for observation but wasn't badly hurt because some of the torn upholstery had formed a protective covering over him.

The woman with the injured legs had been operated on

for serious fractures, and the businessman with chest injuries was in Intensive Care, while the woman who had been found in the toilet was in a stable condition but with severe concussion.

That there had been only the one fatality was amazing, but sadly that wasn't going to be any comfort to the family of the driver of the goods train.

At the end of a day in which she'd been involved in a rail crash and sundry other accidents, had told the man she loved that she would marry him on any terms and been politely turned down, Hannah was ready for an early night.

They hadn't spoken since their conversation in the car and as far as she was concerned that was fine. Kyle had humiliated her once too often and he would be lucky if she looked the side he was on in the future.

But the day's upsets weren't over. There was a handwritten note waiting for her at the unit, and when she read it her jaw dropped.

'Have tracked you down,' it said. 'Should have got details of your whereabouts from you yesterday but the nice lady where you were staying in Cheltenham has given me your work address. I need to see you, Hannah. I've booked into a hotel for a couple of days. Will see you tomorrow...'

All of that was mind-boggling, but it was the signature at the bottom that had her squirming. 'Love, Paul,' it said.

She sank down onto the nearest chair. It was years since she'd heard from her selfish brother-in-law and now he'd butted into her life twice in two days.

He was bent on worming his way back into her affections and typically he was taking it for granted that she would be agreeable.

Ugh! The thought of it. If Kyle saw Paul hanging around what would he think? She shrugged slender shoulders. What did it matter? Why get worked up about it? They weren't going anywhere.

*   *   *

After a restless night, during which her dreams had been a mixture of Kyle trapped in the burning carriage and Paul stalking her, Hannah was listless and heavy-eyed when she arrived at the unit.

The thought that Paul might stroll in at any moment only added to her gloom, and as the day got under way she settled down to await the inevitable.

She would dearly like to know what he was up to. One thing was for sure. Paul wasn't following up Sunday's meeting just to pass the time of day. She could tell that by his note. He would want something of her. He always did. His appearance at the home of Kyle's parents had been for a reason and it wasn't for any of the ones Kyle might have considered.

On impulse she rang Reception on the ground floor of the hospital. 'If anyone asks for me, please don't let them come up here,' she told them. 'I'll come down.'

Which was all very well, as long as he showed up while she was there. But if she'd been called out, what then?

The morning dragged on with Kyle in the office and Graham on first call. The rest of them sat around, ready in case they should be required, with Hannah waiting all the time for the phone to ring.

She should have known better. Paul was a law unto himself.

'Is that guy outside in the passage trying to attract your attention?' Pete asked as he was about to go for an early lunch.

When she looked up Paul was there, waving to her at the other side of the glass partition, and as she got to her feet she thought, All I need now is for Kyle to appear. Even if Paul's appearance was for entirely innocent reasons, it wasn't going to do anything for the mess that was her relationship with Kyle.

For one thing, if Kyle should see them together he would

think that she'd been in touch with Paul since yesterday, as at that time Paul hadn't known how to find her.

As far as Kyle was concerned, the fact that Paul had long since remarried would become a minor issue compared to him having sought her out again so quickly.

She couldn't get out to the passage fast enough. Apart from anything else, members of the public weren't allowed in their part of the building, but that was the least of her worries.

CHAPTER EIGHT

'HANNAH!' Paul cried when she went out into the passage.

Dodging his outstretched arms, she gave him a tight smile and asked, 'What brings you to London, Paul, so soon after the weekend?'

'You, of course.'

'I see. So why don't I take you downstairs into the restaurant for a coffee?'

'Yes, why not?' he said immediately. 'It will give us a chance to make up for what we didn't say then.'

It won't as far as I'm concerned, she thought as she steered him towards the stairs. He was the last person she wanted to talk to.

So far there was no sign of Kyle, but he wasn't going to be in his office for ever and at that moment all she could think of was getting Paul out of sight.

'I can't be long,' she told him as they seated themselves at a table. 'I'm on call all the time.'

He pulled a face. 'Surely you've time to spare for me.'

'I only have time to spare for the sick and injured when I'm on duty,' she explained levelly. 'So, what is it you want of me, Paul? We hadn't seen each other in years until Sunday, and now here you are again. What's the problem? Knowing you, there has to be one.'

'I'm sick, Hannah,' he wailed, 'and you're a doctor. I need your help. It must have been fate that has brought us together again.'

Hannah felt her insides beginning to knot. Please, don't let me be burdened with him again, she pleaded to those same fates.

'What's wrong with you,' she asked with assumed firmness, 'that you have to seek me out when the country is full of doctors? I'm not a GP. My skills are channelled into accident and emergency. I'm sure that your wife would rather you saw a consultant for whatever ails you.'

He pulled a face. 'Angela never has anything wrong with her and has no sympathy for those that have. I've got Parkinson's disease.'

'I see. And what have you done about it?'

'Had some tests and that's what came up.'

'And so what do you expect me to do?'

'Monitor my treatment. Keep an eye on my case.'

She laughed. He was incredible. And what a nerve! He thought that because she'd been there for him the last time there had been trauma in his life, he had only to lift a finger.

She got to her feet. 'I'm afraid there's nothing I can do for you, Paul. I'm sorry that you've got such a debilitating illness, but it's for your GP and the doctors at your local hospital to treat it. They can do far more for you than I can.'

He wasn't listening. He was looking over her shoulder, and when Kyle's voice came from behind like a blast from a Siberian winter she knew the reason for his inattention.

'Have you forgotten that you're on call, Dr Morgan?' he asked with a glacial look in her brother-in-law's direction.

'I'm afraid that I had for the moment,' she confessed.

It was true unfortunately. Only Paul could make her forget why she was on the premises, she thought dismally.

'So we meet again, Templeton,' Paul said smoothly.

Hannah raised her eyes heavenwards. The moment was going from bad to worse.

'So it would appear.'

'As I explained yesterday, Kyle is in charge of the unit,' Hannah butted in hurriedly. 'I'm sorry, Paul, but I have to go. I hope that all goes well in the future, and don't worry

too much about what we've been discussing. There are lots
of ways to keep it under control.'

'Was that his libido you were talking about?' Kyle asked
as they went back to the rooftop.

'Don't be disgusting,' she said coldly.

He gave a dry smile and went on, 'So you've been in
touch since the weekend?'

'No. We haven't.'

'So how did he know where to find you?' he questioned
disbelievingly.

Hannah's sigh had weariness in it.

'Paul is never short on cheek when he wants something.
If you can stop doubting me for a second you might be
able to work out how he got the information.'

'Wherever he got it from, the fact remains that you still
have time for him. Why didn't you tell him to get lost?'

'Would it make any difference if I told you that I did?'
As they stepped out of the lift she asked, 'Was I needed?
Or were you just pulling rank?'

'You were needed inasmuch as I want to know your
whereabouts at all times when you're here. If Pete hadn't
seen you in the restaurant with your brother-in-law I
wouldn't have known where you were, and in our job that
kind of thing is no good.'

'I know, and I'm sorry. But did you have to come and
check us out? You wouldn't have if it had been anyone
else, but because it was Paul—'

'I think I can be forgiven for that,' Kyle said tightly, 'He
was responsible for ruining our lives. Or had you forgotten
that? He has some cheek to come pestering you after all
this time.'

They were back in their own part of the building and the
matter had to rest there, but it didn't stop Kyle from feeling
that there were things left unsaid.

Hannah hadn't told him why that pest had called to see

her. Why he'd sought her out again after Sunday's meeting. She'd been adamant that she hadn't been in touch with him since then, yet...

As crisper autumn days followed the long hot summer, the doctors of the fast response team continued to fulfil their purpose. And if their only female member and the man in charge kept each other at a distance, it was noticed but not commented on.

Some people might have thought that they saw a bit too much of each other, working in the same environment and then going to their respective homes in the same apartment block. If anyone had thought to ask the two participants in the game why they were so cool with each other they might have been surprised.

On Hannah's part there was a determination not to succumb to her feelings for Kyle while he was so dubious of everything about her.

Yet behind it was despair. The weeks were flying by. Soon she would be leaving the team for an appointment in a hospital and the chances of her seeing him then were remote.

She had told him that she would marry him if he wanted her to, no matter what the circumstances, and what had he done? It had been his turn to play hard to get.

He'd been prickly to say the least ever since Paul had appeared on the scene and she was damned if she was going to start justifying herself all over again with regard to her brother-in-law.

She'd explained that their second meeting had not been her idea and had expected Kyle to believe her. Also there had been no further communications from Paul, so what was the problem?

When she asked about Ben and his grandparents it was

a different matter. He was happy to talk about those he loved and it made her feel more out in the cold than ever.

Yet as far as she knew there was no other woman in his life, and there was certainly no man in hers. So what were they playing at?

The assumption that he wasn't interested in anyone else lasted until the night when a long-legged brunette was waiting for him as they all spilled out of the building at sunset.

It was only early evening as their working days were shorter now that the summer had gone. Time to get to the theatre or a cinema. Warm enough for a sail on the Thames. As Hannah watched the strange woman hook her arm in Kyle's she could imagine them doing all of those things together if the way she was looking at him was anything to go by.

'Who's the dish?' Jack asked as Kyle and the stranger got into a taxi.

'I have no idea,' she said stonily, with a sinking feeling that keeping Kyle at a distance might have been a case of cutting off her nose to spite her face.

She spent a restless evening as her imagination ran riot and when they met in the entrance hall of the apartments the following morning she scanned his face as if somewhere written on it would be what he'd been up to the night before.

He was observing her blankly. 'What's the matter, Hannah? Have I got a smut on my nose? Or forgotten to brush my hair?'

She managed a smile. 'No, of course not.' Driven by a force she couldn't resist, she added. 'It's just that I thought you might be turning in later after an evening out.'

'Huh? How do you know I went out for the evening?'

'I...er...saw that someone was waiting for you.'

'Ah. I see. And though you can't be bothered to look the

side I'm on these days, you'd like to know who I was with last night.'

'No. Certainly not.'

'In that case I won't tell you.' And as if they had been merely passing the time of day, he departed with a long easy stride that made her want to run after him and shake him.

She hung back after that, deciding that she wasn't going to catch the same train as him, then ended up late as the next one didn't turn up.

He was talking to the operations officer when she came dashing in, and he looked pointedly at his watch.

'Travel problems, Dr Morgan?' he asked smoothly.

She inclined her head and with what grace she could muster went to get changed.

A traffic accident on the motorway, involving a lorry and a motor cyclist, was the first emergency of the day and Hannah went out on it.

The lorry driver had taken his eyes off the road for a second when his mobile phone had rung, and he'd run into the biker who had been coasting along in front of him.

When she got there she found that the bike was a mangled mess and the man who'd been on it had multiple injuries, while the lorry driver was slumped on the grass verge in deep shock.

Motorway police were diverting traffic and an ambulance was already on the scene. As she examined the injured man a paramedic said, 'He's pretty bad, Doctor. A guy on a bike is in no position to argue with a lorry.'

The shunt from the lorry had pushed him so violently forward that he'd been flung head first over the top of the bike. Looking at the state of his machine, it was hard to decide which had been the lesser of two evils—him being thrown, or ending up amongst what was left of the motorcycle.

His helmet had protected his head from serious injury, but as for the rest of him Hannah had grave concerns. There was a trickle of blood coming from his mouth and nose, and when she eased his helmet off the flesh around the eyes and ears was beginning to swell.

'This man needs to be lifted to hospital with all possible speed, or we're going to lose him,' she told those assisting her. 'So let's get him out of here and airborne.'

At the hospital, Hannah phoned Kyle to report back the situation and told him, 'We're at King's, having just brought in a motorcyclist with multiple injuries. There's also a lorry driver in severe shock. He's being transported by ambulance. I was hanging on for a while to see what the A and E here have to say about the biker. Do you need me for anything?' she asked with a wry smile at the irony of the question.

The day he needed her in any way other than as a substitute mother, or as a doctor working alongside him, she would put the flag up!

Almost as if he'd read her thoughts he said, 'Would it matter if I did? Considering that we work together and live in the same apartment block, we communicate very little these days. Who is to blame for that, do you think?'

'I don't know. Both of us perhaps,' she said with sudden weariness.

'So why don't we spend some quality time together for once?' he suggested casually.

'Meaning?'

'An evening at the theatre. Or a day out. Though that could create problems with the working rotas. So maybe an evening would be best. What do you think?'

'Er…yes…I suppose so,' Hannah said slowly, taken aback at the sudden invitation.

'So when?'

He actually sounded keen, she thought in continuing surprise. Was he going to slot her in when the leggy brunette wasn't available?

She'd only seen him with the woman once, yet she was jealous. It was the way the woman had hooked her arm in his that had sparked it off. As if she had a claim on him. But, then, what was wrong if she had? It was Kyle's own business who he spent his leisure hours with, and surprisingly, at the moment, she was in the frame.

'I don't mind when. I'll leave it to you to choose,' she told him, and thought at the same time that he could be using the phone call to invite her out, rather than asking her face to face. But since when had Kyle Templeton ever been nervous in her presence? The boot was on the other foot.

At that moment the sister in charge of the trauma unit came out into the corridor and Hannah said quickly, 'I'm about to get some news on the injured biker. Do you want to hold on?'

'No. We have some Ministry of Health officials due to visit the unit any time. I'll speak to you when you get back.'

'The patient has head and spinal injuries and is in a serious condition,' the sister told Hannah. 'He's gone for X-rays and will almost certainly go right into Theatre as soon as we get the results. We've been resuscitating him ever since he was brought in and he's only just hanging on.'

Hannah nodded gravely. The news was no better than she'd expected. It was just so sad that a lorry driver should have taken his eyes off the road for a second and ended up being responsible for such a terrible tragedy.

So much for vowing to leave Hannah alone, Kyle thought as he put the phone down. She'd asked him if he needed her and he hadn't been able to resist taking her up on it. Even though he'd been well aware that she was referring to the job, he'd used it as an excuse to ask her out. Surprisingly, it had worked.

He was sick of seeing her all the time and never getting near her. There wasn't a night that passed when he didn't have to restrain himself from going down to her apartment and knocking on her door.

When they'd first met up again it had seemed as if there was a lifetime to put things right between them, but she was already making plans for when the six months were up, checking out vacancies for accident and emergency consultants in the various hospitals.

So far as he knew her enquiries hadn't included anything London-based, which meant that once she'd finished this last part of her training he wouldn't see her any more.

Was she staying clear of work in the capital because of him? he wondered. Because she wanted a clean break? Permanent this time.

Could he cope with that? Letting her out of his sight again? Why hadn't he taken advantage when she'd said she would marry him on any terms, because she'd been so concerned about what Ben's situation would be if anything happened to his father?

If he didn't make the most of this night at the theatre with a special meal afterwards, he was a fool.

At that moment the VIPs he'd been expecting arrived, and if the efficient head of the helicopter medical service seemed preoccupied as he showed them round, it was thought to be due to the budgeting economies that they were contemplating.

'Which show would you like to see?' he asked Hannah when she arrived back at base.

'*Joseph and His Amazing Technicolor Dreamcoat*,' she said immediately. 'I believe it's on somewhere in the city. I saw it once long ago and loved it.'

He'd smiled and for a moment Hannah felt that all their

differences were forgotten. They were just two people who wanted to be with each other. At least that was how she felt. Kyle was his usual enigmatic self, but she consoled herself with the thought that he wouldn't have asked her out if it wasn't what he wanted.

'So you're sure that any night I can get tickets for is all right with you?' he was asking.

She nodded, realising that he would deduce from that just how full her social calendar was.

As she turned away he called her back. 'Ben is coming to stay with me over the weekend. Mum and Dad have been invited to stay with friends in Henley for a couple of days. It's the couple's silver wedding. So they're going to drop Ben off here on the way.'

Hannah's face lit up.

'Am I likely to see anything of him?'

Kyle smiled.

'Yes, if that's what you want. How would you like to come house-hunting with us?'

'I'd love to,' she said with unconscious wistfulness.

'Is Saturday afternoon all right? I'll make some appointments with house agents.'

'Yes, fine,' she agreed.

At least it would be if she was in on it, instead of being cast in the role of interested onlooker.

Some of the regular staff on the unit had been asking Hannah where she intended moving to when she'd finished her training, but she'd had to tell them that as yet she didn't know.

Pete and Graham were two of them, along with Jack, whose affair with a receptionist from Harley Street was over.

He was back on her case, asking her out all the time and accepting her refusals with his usual good nature.

'I thought that you and the chief had something going a while back,' he said one day when they shared a table in the staff dining room, 'but I get the feeling that it has sunk without trace.'

He couldn't have put it more aptly, Hannah thought as she declined to answer, but thankfully there might be a relaunch in the offing, in the form of an afternoon spent with Kyle and Ben and a night out at the theatre.

'I've booked the theatre tickets for a week on Friday,' Kyle informed Hannah the following day. 'Is that all right with you?'

She smiled across at him. 'Yes. That will be fine. I'm looking forward to it.'

'Me, too,' he said, his voice softening.

They were outside in the passage and at that moment were alone. Suddenly it was there, the force that had lain dormant ever since the night in his parents' garden. Oblivious to their surroundings, uncaring that any second they might be interrupted, they moved towards each other. As Kyle took her in his arms and claimed her mouth with his, Hannah gave herself up to the moment.

It was doomed from the start. It had to be, because of where they were. Within seconds they could hear voices and footsteps approaching and he had to release her. But their glances still held, unable to let go.

'We've got a call-out, Hannah,' Jack said suddenly from behind her. Bringing herself back from some far-away place, she nodded.

'Ambulance services say there's been a shotgun wounding in the East End and we're needed pronto,' he informed her.

'I'll see you folks later, then,' Kyle said briskly, and as if they had been doing nothing more than passing the time of day he strolled into the operations room.

'You look a trifle flustered, Dr Morgan,' the pilot said as they took off. 'Am I to take it that you were involved in a "fast response" of your own when I interrupted just then?'

'You could say that.'

'Ah! So you and the boss are back on again! It's easy to see that he has his sights on you, but I wasn't sure if you felt the same.'

'What do you mean—Kyle having his sights on me?'

'I mean that he never takes his eyes off you.'

'Rubbish. That's because he doesn't trust me.'

She'd said it jokingly, but it brought her down to earth. The fact that they could melt towards each other as they just had didn't mean that Kyle really had put the past behind him. She hadn't forgotten the look on his face when he'd seen Paul sitting opposite her in the hospital restaurant.

But there wasn't time for speculating. Jack was about to bring the Eurocopter down onto waste ground beside an East End pub that was surrounded by police. If that and the flashing lights of an ambulance were anything to go by, there was big trouble down below.

'Looks like a shoot out,' the paramedic who was with her said apprehensively.

They were touching down at that moment and Hannah stared at him. 'I was under the impression that the shooting had already taken place and we've been called out to treat the victim.'

'Yes, but there wouldn't be so many police about if it was all over.'

The man who'd been shot was lying in the pub car park with ambulance staff bending over him. As they hurried towards them a senior police officer blocked their way.

'We have a dangerous situation here, Doctor,' he said. 'The gunman is holed up inside the public house and he's got the landlord and his wife as hostages, so we daren't rush the place.'

'I see,' she said slowly, 'but that shouldn't affect us, should it? Once I've treated the man we'll airlift him out with all speed. So if you'll excuse me…'

There was no time to be standing, talking. The victim could be dying at this very minute, she thought as she ran to where he lay.

He'd been running away and the blast had almost missed him. As it was, there was some damage to his shoulder, but the rest of him seemed to be intact. Which was a minor miracle, knowing the injuries such a weapon could inflict.

Conscious, and obviously in a state of terror, he moaned, 'Don't let him come near me. He tried to kill me! We were getting ready for opening and the landlord was about to go to the bank. He'd just taken yesterday's takings out of the safe when this guy appeared from nowhere, waving a gun. He told us all to lie on the floor, but I was nearest to the door and I panicked and ran outside. That was when he shot me.'

The ambulance man with him nodded. 'Luckily some guy was going past with a mobile and he phoned us and the police.'

'You don't need to worry about being attacked again,' Hannah told her patient. 'The gunman won't be going anywhere for a while. He's inside the pub with the landlord and his wife and the place is surrounded.

'You're lucky. Part of your shoulder caught the blast, but it could have been a lot worse if he'd got you full on.'

As she opened her kit to treat him a voice from inside the public house bellowed, 'There's a woman in here, chokin'. If blondie's a doctor you'd better send her in.'

Hannah got to her feet and picked up her bag. 'You carry on here,' she told the paramedic. 'It looks as if I'm needed elsewhere.'

Suddenly a burly, bald-headed man opened the door. His face was as white as a sheet and he cried, 'She's having an asthma attack. You've got to send the doc in to my missus. She's going to die if you don't!'

Hannah didn't wait for permission. She'd seen fatalities from severe asthma attacks in the past and couldn't stand by to let it happen again when there was something she could do.

She was quaking inside but her step didn't falter as she went through the front door. It was dark inside and it took a few seconds for her to focus. When she did the first thing she saw was a slim youth holding a shotgun.

His hands were trembling and Hannah thought, The crazy young fool. He's more nervous than I am.

The landlord was at her elbow, pulling her towards a room at the back of the bar, and as she followed him she could hear the harsh, rasping breaths of the asthmatic woman.

There was cyanosis present. Her face and lips were blue, her skin pale and clammy. Those symptoms alone were sufficient for Hannah to assess the seriousness of the attack.

'Has she used her bronchodilator?' she asked of the frantic husband.

'Yes!' he cried. 'But it's done no good.'

'We'll repeat the dose,' she said quickly, 'and if that doesn't work a fast trip to hospital is going to be needed.'

The lad had come to stand behind them, cradling the gun in the crook of his arm. When he heard that he cried, 'You ain't taking 'er out of here.'

'Do you want two deaths on your conscience?' Hannah asked levelly as she prepared to give the patient a straight injection instead of trusting the slower relief of the inhaler.

He blanched. 'Why, is the cellar man dead?'

It seemed the right moment to exaggerate and so she said, 'Not yet, but shotgun injuries often end up fatal and none of these people have done you any harm. I'm going to tell my assistant to send the man you shot to hospital by ambulance, and the lady will be going by helicopter.'

The youth's face lightened. 'Now, that's different. The chopper—of course. You can give me a lift at the same time.'

'What?'

'I'm coming with you, Doc.'

Suddenly he was macho man, his panic forgotten. 'I'll tell you where I want dropping off. So let's get moving, shall we?'

The landlord's wife was beginning to breath more easily but she was still in great distress and every time her eyes fixed on the shotgun she started to choke all over again.

'Walk her to the chopper,' the youth commanded, adding with a glance at the sweating landlord, 'He can stay here. There won't be room for him.'

'First of all I have to tell my assistant that we're going to need the helicopter and that he has to send the injured man by road,' she insisted.

'And while you're doing it you can tell the coppers to keep back as we make our way towards it…or I might get trigger-happy.'

'I'm all right' she told the fraught paramedic when he answered his mobile, 'but you'll have to send your patient by road. We need to get the lady to hospital as quickly as possible… And will you tell the police that our young gun-man is travelling with us and demands that they stay well back, or—'

'He'll shoot you!' he croaked. 'The boss is on his way and is he mad…'

Mad? Hannah thought absently. Why was Kyle mad? She was doing what she was paid for—treating the sick.

The rest of what he had to say was lost as the phone was

snatched out of her hand. 'Come on, then, Doc,' the lad said. 'Get her movin'.'

With the woman leaning heavily on Hannah and wheezing noisily with every step, they made their way to where the helicopter was waiting. The police were hovering like beasts ready to pounce on their prey, but having heard the message from the gunman they made no move.

As the door of the helicopter slid open Hannah's eyes widened. It wasn't Jack or his copilot looking down on them. Someone else had arrived at the scene while she'd been inside the public house and she immediately felt less afraid.

There was grim purpose in the glance meeting hers and a tightness of jaw that told her Kyle wasn't about to let their helicopter be taken over by a gunman.

'This lady needs urgent hospital treatment,' she said quickly. 'And the young man with the gun wants a lift.'

Kyle smiled. 'Sure thing, Dr Morgan. But let's get the patient on board first, shall we?'

The lad had his back to them, menacing the police with the shotgun while they were helping the patient on board. But as soon as Hannah had followed her he swivelled round, ready to join them. It was then that he met the toe of Kyle's boot right on the chin.

With a howl of pain he dropped the gun and then it was all over. Before he could retrieve his weapon Kyle was on him, with the police close behind. Within minutes he was handcuffed and being pushed into the back seat of one of the police cars.

'Anchors away, then,' Kyle said smoothly, as if disarming a gunman was part of a day's work. As they began lifting off from the car park the reality of what she had just been part of hit Hannah.

To find Kyle there at a time when they'd all been in such danger was something she would never forget. All right, it was all part and parcel of the job, but if the way he was looking at her was anything to go by, he was someone who had just been to hell and back.

He might be putting on a calm front for the sick woman and the other members of his staff, but it was there in his eyes, the knowledge that she could have been killed at any moment since entering the public house.

CHAPTER NINE

WHEN the paramedic had phoned to say that Hannah had gone into the public house where the armed robber was holding a publican and his wife hostage, Kyle's face whitened.

'Why, for God's sake?' he'd barked.

'The landlady is in a bad way. She's having a serious asthma attack and the gunman asked that Dr Morgan go in to attend to her.'

'And the police let her?'

'They had no choice. She was in there before they could do anything about it. I've sent the injured man to hospital on her instructions. He wasn't too serious, and we're keeping the helicopter for the asthma patient.'

'I'm on my way,' Kyle had said abruptly, 'and tell the police if anything happens to her they'll have me to deal with.'

The chill of dread had been upon him. He felt as if his blood had turned to ice. The fellow in the pub had already shot one person. Supposing…!

He daren't think about it. Not Hannah. Beautiful, uncomplicated Hannah, whose life he'd messed up a long time ago and who was still running round in circles because of him.

All right, it was what their job was all about, treating the sick and suffering, but not while looking down the barrel of a shotgun!

Please, don't let anything happen to her! he'd prayed as with siren blaring he wove in and out of the traffic. He couldn't even contemplate losing Hannah.

147

The public house had come in sight at last and he'd
realised that with the helicopter still there and the police
presence she must be still inside the building.

'I'm from the unit that Dr Morgan works for,' he said
as he flung himself out of the car. 'What's happening?'

The policeman he was addressing had wasted no time in
telling him. 'As far as we know, the doctor is safe. She's
about to come out with the sick lady and the gunman,
who's demanding a lift in the helicopter.'

Relief had swept over him. So far Hannah was in one
piece, but there was still a man with a gun hovering over
her.

'I'm going on board,' he told the policeman, and before
the man could argue he'd climbed into the helicopter.

'Here they come, sir!' the paramedic had cried, and Kyle
had looked up to see Hannah supporting the gasping
woman as they moved slowly towards them, the gunman
bringing up the rear.

'I'm going to try to disarm him once Dr Morgan and the
woman are on board,' he told Jack. 'There's no way that
thug is setting foot on here. If it goes wrong, or anything
happens to me, don't wait. Take off immediately.'

For once having nothing cheerful to say, the pilot nodded
grimly and then, almost before Kyle had finished speaking,
it was time to act.

When they touched down at the nearest hospital with the
sick woman Hannah gave Kyle a tremulous smile as they
helped their patient out of the helicopter, but his face remained grave.

He'd barely spoken during the flight and it had been left
to Jack and the others to express their relief that the gunman
had been disarmed and in such a manner.

'Talk about never a dull moment,' the copilot had said.
'I wouldn't change this job for anything.'

But it hadn't tempted Kyle to join in. He'd just sat staring alternately at Hannah or out of the window with the ravaged expression that had been on his face ever since they'd been airborne, and now she was trying to get through to him.

Hannah wanted to tell him how much it had meant to her, seeing him there at the door of the helicopter, and that her love for him was deep and strong, but he wasn't tuned in. She could tell.

'What possessed you to do such a thing?' he said roughly, finding his voice at last. 'That lunatic could have killed you!'

'Yes, I know,' she said, backing away. 'But what was I supposed to do? Let the landlord's wife choke to death? You would have done the same.'

'Yes, of course I would, but—'

'There's a different set of rules for you, is there?' she flared.

'Yes. Because, in case you've forgotten, I'm in charge and I'm responsible for the safety of the rest of you. When it comes to myself I have no one to answer to.'

'What about Ben?' she cried. 'He depends on you, doesn't he?'

'I'm talking about the unit,' he snapped. 'Not my private life.'

'I've had enough of this, Kyle,' she said wearily. 'Whatever I do is never right in your eyes. Fortunately my time with the helicopter service is nearly up and I won't be sorry to go.'

His face darkened, but at that moment the doctor who'd taken over the treatment of their patient appeared and spoke quietly to Kyle.

'I'm going to be here for a while,' Kyle said to Hannah. 'You can carry on back to base with Jack and the others. I'll get a taxi.'

'Fine,' she told him frostily.

*   *   *

When Kyle arrived at the unit an hour later, he found Hannah in the centre of a laughing group with glasses of champagne in their hands.

'Here's the other hero of the hour!' someone cried as a glass was thrust into his hand.

Another voice shouted, 'What a woman, eh, sir? Facing up to a guy with a gun!'

'Yes, indeed,' he said grimly. 'But you wouldn't have all been knocking back the drink if Hannah had been killed.'

He saw that he'd wiped the smile off her face and knew he was being a killjoy, but he was still being driven by the memory of the sick terror that had claimed him when he'd heard what she'd got herself involved in. It had been as if a clammy hand had been squeezing his heart and he would remember it to his dying day. And then what had he come back to? A celebration!

How could Kyle treat her like that? Hannah thought wretchedly as she slumped onto the sofa in her sitting room that evening. She'd only joined in the general euphoria to please the others.

In actual fact she'd been feeling shaky and tearful. She'd needed Kyle's calm strength to bring her back to normality, his arms around her as proof that she'd really been safe. And what had she got?

A dressing-down that had made her feel totally irresponsible. All she needed now was for it to be in the newspapers and he really would blow his top.

She didn't understand why he was so peeved at what she'd done. Hadn't he admitted that he would have done the same? It was like she'd told him. There was one set of rules for her and one for him.

He'd only ever pulled rank on her twice. The first time had been when he'd caught her with Paul in the restaurant and reminded her that she was on call, and the second had been today.

Hannah closed her eyes wearily. Why did she keep going back for more when every time their paths crossed it was a disaster? She'd lived without him before and she could do it again, she decided. He was only on the fringe of her life as it was, but from now on he wasn't even going to be that close.

Her head was throbbing, and after taking a painkiller she went to lie on the bed. As she drifted into an exhausted sleep her last thought was that he could take someone else to the theatre as she certainly wasn't going.

The phone awakened her and it was Kyle's voice that came over the line.

Hannah stared at the receiver blearily. Was he ringing to apologise? Or to carry on the grand telling off?

It was neither.

'It's part of my function to ask members of staff if they need counselling after any sort of distressing incident,' he said tonelessly. 'Would you like me to arrange it?'

She was fully awake now and smarting. 'Which distressing incident are you referring to?' she flared. 'The robbery at the public house, or my boss's reaction to it?'

'Don't be clever, Hannah,' he said brusquely. 'You must be blind if you don't know what that was all about.'

'Maybe I am,' she snapped back, 'and with regard to your offer of counselling…no, thanks. I'm not in the market for any favours. And while I'm on that subject, I suggest you find someone else to take to the theatre.'

'Now you're being childish.'

'That's good, coming from you!'

He ignored the comment. 'You'll change your mind about the theatre once you've calmed down.'

'I wouldn't bank on it. I wish my time was up already

so that I didn't have to see you again.' And with an angry click she put the phone down.

At the other end of the line Kyle stared at the receiver, grim-faced. So much for that, he thought.

The most lucid and articulate of men, he couldn't understand why when it came to Hannah Morgan he couldn't talk sense. He'd turned her courageous act into a breach of discipline, and if the rapport between them had been fragile before, now it was non-existent.

All he'd had to do had been to tell her how horrified he'd been about her safety during the pub siege and how his anguish had turned to frustrated anger when he'd seen her drinking champagne as if nothing had happened.

At that moment the phone rang, breaking into his sombre thoughts. He picked it up quickly, hoping that Hannah might have had a change of heart, but it was his mother on the line with Ben chattering in the background.

'A certain little boy would like a word with you,' she said laughingly.

'When I see you on Saturday can I have a new bike, Daddy?' Ben asked without preamble, adding with continuing brevity, 'Without stabilisers.'

Kyle found himself joining in his mother's laughter. 'I think we might be able to manage the bike,' he told him, 'but I'll have to have a think about the stabilisers.'

There was an ache around his heart as he listened to Ben talking about what he'd been doing at school and how he and Grandad had been playing cricket in the garden.

His relationship with Hannah was at an all-time low, but he had to be grateful that Ben still loved him and needed his presence in his life, and if his dreams of the three of them becoming a family came to nothing, then...

His face twisted. Then...what?

*   *   *

Pete Stubbs's wife was pregnant and he was overjoyed. It seemed that they'd wanted children for a long time and none had been forthcoming, but now nature, with its many caprices, was favouring them.

As Hannah watched him accepting the congratulations of the other men on the unit there was sadness in her smile. Would she ever have children with someone she loved? Not if it was up to Kyle. He seemed to go out of his way to keep them apart.

The man in question appeared at that moment. He was late, having been to a resources meeting, and she couldn't tell if the frown on his face was the aftermath of listening to budgeting suggestions or the sight of the thorn in his side in the form of herself.

'Pete's going to be a daddy, Kyle,' Graham told him as the father-to-be smiled across at them.

That wiped the frown off Kyle's face and he went across to Pete and shook his hand. 'Brilliant news, Pete,' he said warmly. 'You'll make a great dad.'

Just as you are yourself, my prickly love, Hannah thought, and if it wasn't for that same prickliness we might have had some babies of our own.

Was he reading her thoughts again? Dark, inscrutable eyes were locking with her own uncomplicated blue gaze, and as if yesterday had never been he was sending out signals.

Not of desire this time. It was a different kind of need that she sensed in him, but she wasn't sure what it stemmed from.

Hannah turned away. She'd given up trying to read his mind. If she had any sense she would have given up on him long ago. But the fact remained that just a little time spent with Kyle was more precious than a one-to-one relationship with anyone else.

'So? Am I forgiven?' he asked when he managed to catch her on her own. He wasn't exactly pleading, but there was an expression on his face that might have been anxiety.

Hannah was tempted to tell him that he was, as he'd been right in some of the things he'd said and, loving him as she did and having wasted so much time, she wanted them to be in harmony, if nothing else.

But that sort of truce would only last until the next time he found her wanting. So she fought down the tenderness that his words had aroused in her and told him, 'As you said yesterday, you're the boss here and, that being so, are entitled to comment when we step out of line. So let's forget it, shall we?'

It was an ungracious sort of reply to Kyle's plea for forgiveness, but in all the months since they'd found each other again she'd never felt more strongly that she had to tread carefully.

'Hmm,' he growled. 'So that's how you feel?'

Her smile was wry.

'Yes, that's how I feel,' she fibbed, and as a call came through at that moment for assistance at the scene of a traffic accident, Hannah was denied the opportunity to say more, even if she'd wanted to.

That same day Kyle had a visitor and Hannah immediately recognised her as the woman who had been waiting for him that night after work when they'd gone off together in a taxi.

This time she'd come up to the helipad to find him, and when Hannah saw how his face brightened at the sight of her, a day that had started well with the news of Pete's forthcoming fatherhood seemed to be going downhill fast.

What had this woman got that she hadn't? she asked herself. Well, Kyle for one thing, if his pleasure at seeing her was anything to go by.

With a quick glance towards Hannah Kyle said, 'I'm going out for a couple of hours. If anyone wants me it will have to wait until I get back.'

There was a telephone call but it was for her. She'd applied for a position in Manchester and was being asked to go for an interview during the following week.

The vacancy was one of three that she was interested in. The other two were in Newcastle-on-Tyne and Gloucestershire.

If Hannah had heard Kyle's visitor speak and noted her accent, part of the mystery would have become clear. Annie Cousins was an Australian on holiday in the UK.

The knowledge might not have brought much comfort, but it would at least have explained where she had materialised from in the monastic life of the busy head of the helicopter emergency services.

'So you're flying back tomorrow,' Kyle said as they faced each other across a table in a nearby wine bar.

''Fraid so,' his visitor said with a pout of full red lips. 'Brad will be sending a search party out for me if I don't go back soon.'

'And you've sorted all the loose ends?'

'Yeah. The estate will be finally wound up this afternoon. It's been a long and complicated business, but that's what comes of marrying a pommie.'

Annie was observing him from beneath long mascara'd lashes.

'Mind you, I could be persuaded to stay. It only needs a word from a certain person that they're going to miss me and I'll cancel the airline ticket.'

Kyle shook his head. 'Your place is back home, Annie. Brad needs you.'

'And you don't?'

'Not in that way. For one thing I have Ben to think about, and for another I have unfinished business with someone who's going to need a lot of convincing.'

'You're in love with somebody else?'

He smiled. 'Yes, but I've a feeling I have a long way to go before she'll believe me.'

'If she has any trouble with that just tell her that I'm there on the sidelines. It's surprising how we all place more value on someone that somebody else wants.'

Kyle's smile had a tinge of sadness. He didn't want to be wanted because someone else had designs on him.

'There'll be someone for you back home, Annie,' he assured her. 'You're an attractive woman…and if what you say is true, you'll soon be a rich one.'

She shrugged narrow shoulders. 'Looks like it, but…'

'What?'

'I'll never know whether I'm loved for my money or myself.' She got to her feet. 'With you I would have known that it wasn't the money.'

Her red lips brushed his fleetingly. 'Bye, Kyle.'

When Kyle came back on to the unit he was smiling and Hannah's spirits plummeted even further.

He saw her expression and asked, 'What's wrong?'

She shook her head listlessly. 'Nothing.'

But something was very wrong. The woman he'd just left had made it clear on the two occasions that Hannah had seen her with him that Kyle was more than just a friend. Maybe he felt the same way. She had to know.

'Actually, I was wondering about that woman you saw today.'

Kyle's smile faded, slightly. 'Annie Cousins is an Australian, the widow of an English friend of mine who died a year ago. And before you ask—I'm not interested in

her. She's going back home tomorrow to her teenage son.
Annie has been over here to sort out her husband's estate
and is going to be a rich woman.'

'And that didn't tempt you?'

Kyle wasn't smiling at all now.

'I thought you knew me better than that, Hannah.'

'Yes. I do,' she said contritely. 'I'm sorry, Kyle. We're
involved in a war of words again. I don't know why it's
always like this!'

'Nor do I. Maybe one day we'll get it right.'

As the phone on his desk began to ring she murmured
dismally, 'Yes. Maybe we will.'

Friday was one of the busiest days since Hannah had joined
the team. As they found themselves dealing with a spate of
traffic accidents, victims of crime and every other medical
emergency that might require the services of the fast response teams, it seemed as if a mischievous force was
abroad on the streets of the city.

With Kyle's mysterious woman friend accounted for,
Hannah was feeling happier, and when he'd reminded her
about their house-hunting on Saturday afternoon and the
theatre date on the following Friday, she hadn't repeated
her earlier refusal.

Pete and Graham were on leave, and when a call came
in for a doctor to treat the victim of a house fire, Kyle went
himself, leaving Hannah and Charles to cover any further
emergencies that might come through during his absence.

They hadn't long to wait. He'd no sooner gone than a
call came in from a road accident in Kensington. As
Charles had only just got back from a previous call-out,
Hannah said she would take it.

She was using a car as Jack had taken Kyle to the house
fire in the Eurocopter, and it was as she was driving towards

Kensington that it came through on the radio that a helicopter had crashed in a field beside the motorway.

'Oh, no!' she cried in horror. 'Don't let it be ours...
please!'

The area where it had come down wasn't far from where
Kyle had gone to the house fire, and dread had Hannah in
its grip. There would be four of them on board, all of them
dedicated to saving life wherever possible. Jack and his
copilot, the paramedic...and Kyle. Who would be there to
save theirs if it was the Eurocopter that had come down?

Instinct told her to turn around and go to where the crash
had taken place, but that would be leaving a critically injured motorist at risk and she couldn't do that. Kyle
wouldn't want her to in any case.

So she drove on, fear making her blood run cold. If anything had happened to him she would want to die, too, but
that wouldn't do, would it?

She'd told Kyle that she would marry him because of
something like this happening. So that Ben would never be
left an orphan.

But deep down she knew she should have told him the
real reason. That she loved him utterly and completely. He
might have taken more notice of that.

The motorist was elderly and of an age when he shouldn't
have been driving, a fact that would have been brought
home to him had he been conscious.

He had careered off the road and onto the pavement,
hitting a tree in the process. Fortunately there had been no
other vehicles involved or injuries to pedestrians, but the
driver himself was in a serious condition, due to his age
and the force with which he'd struck the tree.

Severe facial and chest injuries were the main concern,
and because of that he was having difficulty breathing,

Hannah inserted a tube into his lungs to help his breathing and gave him an injection to reduce the pain just as the ambulance arrived.

'We could have done with the helicopter here,' she told the crew as they stretchered the pensioner into the ambulance, 'but it's out on another call. Or at least it was. I've just heard on my radio that a helicopter has crashed.'

'It won't be Jack,' one of the ambulance crew said. 'That guy could fly a chopper in his sleep.'

'I hope you're right,' she said soberly.

After she'd radioed ahead to Accident and Emergency at the nearest hospital, Hannah made her way towards base with mouth dry and heart thumping.

Every minute was like a lifetime until she heard a familiar roar up above. When she looked up it was there, the Eurocopter, flying back to base.

Kyle was safe. They all were. Theirs wasn't the only helicopter in use in the city and the crash meant sorrow for someone, but thank goodness the staff of the emergency service weren't involved.

In those moments she realised that worry over a loved one affected people in different ways. In Kyle's case it had erupted in frustrated anger and she should have made allowances for it.

It was strange that only twenty-four hours later she'd had to face up to the same dreadful kind of anxiety. They should both be grateful that the fates had been kind to them, and when she saw him next she would tell him that she understood.

When she got back to the operations room there wasn't a doctor in sight. Charles had been called out while she'd been out and as yet there was no sign of the helicopter and its occupants.

She was chatting to the operations officer with a mug of

hot tea in her hand when they came striding in with Kyle at the forefront.

He came straight across and, observing her blotched face, said, 'What's wrong? You've been crying.'

'Today it was my turn to be involved in a nightmare,' she said contritely. 'I heard on the radio that a helicopter had crashed in the area where you'd gone and I thought that...' Her voice faltered as the horror of it came back.

He said gently, 'You thought that it was us.'

'Yes, I did, and, Kyle...'

'Hmm?'

'I'm sorry that I was so insensitive to your anxiety yesterday. I guess that we all have different ways of shedding tension.'

'You with tears and me blowing my top?'

'Something like that.'

'So we're friends again?'

'Yes.'

He was smiling. 'Good. Let's hope the truce lasts a bit longer this time...and by the way, having actually seen the crash and realised that any survivors might need our services more than the call we'd gone out on, I radioed Charles to go to the house fire emergency while Jack landed us beside the wreck of the chopper. It belonged to a wealthy businessman who was on his way to an appointment. Both he and his secretary were killed. The pilot was the only survivor and I was able to treat him on the spot for heart failure and burns.'

'Burns?'

'Yes, the cabin was on fire.'

She shuddered. 'You didn't...?'

'We were the first on the scene, before the fire brigade or the ambulance, so what do you think?'

'You went inside.'

'It was just a matter of seconds to drag him out. We could see that it was too late for the other two.'

'And I suppose that as you're in charge of the outfit it was all right for you to do that.'

He was smiling. 'Point taken. And now if there's any tea going I wouldn't mind having some. Going into burning helicopters is thirsty work.' Hannah shuddered again. 'Don't worry. It was only a matter of minutes before the fire brigade arrived.'

'Don't make light of it,' she said raggedly. 'I was so relieved when I knew that it wasn't the Eurocopter that had crashed, but now you're bringing all the horror of it back by telling me about the risks you took.'

'So you care enough to be worried about me?' Kyle asked in a low voice.

'Of course I do!' she said levelly, and if he was expecting anything more personal in front of Jack and the paramedic he was in for a disappointment.

'I worry about everyone on the fast response teams,' she went on. 'It's dangerous work, very dangerous sometimes. Yet I've never heard any of the regulars say they want to quit.'

'That's so,' he agreed, 'but with regard to the likes of yourself, the ships that pass in the night, I believe you have an interview in Manchester next week. Why didn't you tell me?'

'I didn't think you'd be interested.'

'Thanks a bunch,' he said sarcastically. 'By the time you go we will have worked together for almost six months and you don't think I'm bothered where you go from here.'

'That's right.'

He ignored that.

'Why aren't you trying to get a placement in London? Is it because you don't want to be near me? That having been thrown into my company here, whether you liked it or not, you now want to put as big a distance as you can between us?'

'The interview in Manchester is just one of a few,' she told him, 'and you can hardly say that you'll be weeping on my shoulder when I go. So why all the fuss?'

'I'm not fussing,' he said quietly. 'I'm just trying to see into your mind.'

'Don't bother, Kyle. You might see things there that you don't want to know about.'

'I would be the judge of that.'

'Like you passed judgement on me long ago?'

'I have no answer to that,' he said. Unzipping the front of his surgical suit, he made his way to the locker room.

CHAPTER TEN

WHEN Kyle and Ben called for her on Saturday afternoon Hannah's spirits rose.

She'd been longing to see the child again and now he was here, eyeing her shyly and looking just a little bit too scrubbed and clean.

'Hello, Ben,' she said softly. 'It's lovely to see you again.'

He was smiling now. 'We've just been to buy a new bike, Hannah…without stabilisers.'

'Great,' she enthused, feeling that Kyle might have thought that at seven years old Ben wouldn't need them. 'When your dad buys this new house that he's looking for, he'll have to make sure that there's plenty of room for you to ride your bike, won't he?'

He nodded gravely. 'Yes, I'd like that, but I won't know anyone in London, will I, Hannah?'

She agreed with him on that, but wasn't going to voice her reservations.

'You'll soon make friends,' she said gently, 'and wherever I'm working I'll come to see you.'

'Yes, but you won't be there to take me to school and give me my breakfast.'

Kyle's expression was just as grave as his son's and Hannah was glad that he wasn't going to answer Ben's questions with assumed heartiness.

'*I'll* be there,' he said, 'or the nice housekeeper that I'm going to find for us.'

You could have had me! Hannah's rebellious blue gaze said, but just as he read the message in her glance so she understood that his bland regard was his way of telling her that the idea had been considered and discarded.

Don't let Kyle put you off, she told herself. Forget everything else and enjoy the time with Ben. Maybe they won't find a house today, and the longer it is before they do, the less Ben will worry about it.

Kyle had picked up a stack of brochures, but the only one he was interested in was a big family-type house backing onto Wimbledon Common.

'It's a bit big for just the two of you, isn't it?' Hannah questioned when they pulled up in front of a gabled house with the spacious dignity of a bygone age.

The bland expression was still in place as he said easily, 'Better too big than too small. Just forget the size of it, Hannah, and tell me what you think.'

'It's lovely,' she breathed. 'Ben would have a super time in those huge gardens. To someone like myself who hasn't had a proper home in years, a place like this is paradise.'

'And that's before you've been inside,' he said whimsically as the estate agent came bustling out to meet them.

As they went from room to room Hannah's spirits dropped lower and lower. What was she doing here? Inflicting punishment upon herself? And why had Kyle asked her to come? He'd already said that a housekeeper was going to rule the roost.

The master bedroom, decorated in the palest of creams and gold, was the room that she was least anxious to see and when the agent turned to Kyle and said with a look in her direction, 'I'm sure that you and your wife will agree this is a truly beautiful room.' Hannah went out onto the landing, deciding that if the man thought her rude it was just too bad.

On the way home, with Ben beside her in the back seat of the hire car, Hannah put the blues to one side and gave her full attention to the little boy who had forgotten his earlier worries and was chattering excitedly about the new house.

Kyle hadn't made any further comments regarding it and she wasn't going to ask, but there had been a sense of purpose about him all the time they'd been viewing that had told her his mind was already made up.

'Let's go and find something to eat, shall we?' he said, breaking into her thoughts. And with Ben chirping his agreement, Hannah prepared to enjoy what time was left with the two people she loved the most.

It was the Wednesday of the following week and Hannah's interview in the great northern city was over. It had been clear that the position as a consultant in accident and emergency in a busy hospital in the centre of Manchester could be hers if she wanted it, but that was the trouble. Did she want it?

There had been no further comments from Kyle regarding the interview, but his earlier remarks were imprinted on her mind. Why wasn't she looking for a position in London? he'd wanted to know. Was it because she didn't want to be near him?

To be near him was all she'd ever asked for, but not under the conditions that prevailed at present. Yet as she strolled through the gardens in Piccadilly, beneath the lesser warmth of a late autumn sun, there was no enthusiasm in her.

All around were apartments. Expensive modern developments, many of them on the various waterfronts of the Manchester Ship Canal. They were impressive, and for those employed in the city a convenience not to be sneezed at. She supposed that it would be in one of these that she would live if she took the position.

But all the time in her mind's eye she was seeing a house in Wimbledon with gracious rooms and gardens that would be like paradise to a small boy. Compared to that, a modern, red-brick apartment came a poor second.

As a tram, that was part of the city's Metro Link system glided to a stop beside her, *en route* for the railway station she boarded it, having already decided that she didn't want the job.

She would be out on a limb here in Manchester when her heart was somewhere else.

'How did the interview go?' were Kyle's first words on Thursday morning.

'Good. I think.'

'So you might take it, if it's offered?'

Hannah shook her head. 'I don't think so.'

His face lightened but his next remark was brusque.

'Why?'

'I've already worked in Manchester. I'd rather go to somewhere new.'

'I see. So it's wait-and-see time, is it?'

She smiled. 'Yes, it is.'

'About tomorrow night,' he said, changing the subject. 'I'm going to be out for most of the day and won't be coming back here. The show starts at seven-thirty, so I'll pick you up at your apartment at seven if that's all right. Will it give you enough time after leaving here?'

'Just about.'

'Good. I'll see you then.'

For the rest of the day Kyle's step was light and he didn't have to look far for the reason. Hannah wasn't going to Manchester!

The thought that she might have interviews in other far-flung places he put firmly to the back of his mind. The news was great, and as a fitting climax to a good week tomorrow they were going to the theatre.

For once he was determined to say the right thing and

he was hoping that the right answer might be forthcoming. The fact that he was going to be embroiled in meetings for most of Friday was a minor inconvenience compared to what he had to look forward to in the evening.

This would be their first real date in years Hannah thought as Friday took its course, and she had a feeling deep down that it was going to be the most important one…ever.

The unit was quiet during the morning, but in the early afternoon, as was often the case, it began to hot up, with calls coming in all the time and the staff having to decide which should be given the priority of the helicopter.

None of them knew that the petite blonde doctor and their boss had an engagement for that evening, so it wasn't surprising that when a call came in shortly before sunset they left Hannah to deal with it because she was the first doctor on call for the day.

Hannah glanced anxiously at the clock when the call came through. Normally she would be leaving in half an hour, but with the kind of emergency that had been reported there was no telling how long she would be, and as the others had all drifted off home she couldn't ask for a favour.

Jack wasn't too thrilled either as he also had plans for the evening, but with his usual good humour he was ready to lift off within minutes, once the fire crew had checked him over.

Kyle might still be in his meeting, she thought as she picked up a surgical kit. It would only take a second to warn him that she might be late. But when she rang through to headquarters she was told that he'd gone and would be somewhere on his way home at that moment.

There was no answer from his mobile when she tried to get through, and as the pilots were getting fidgety there was nothing else she could do but climb aboard and hope that he might see the Eurocopter in the sky and phone in to check on her whereabouts.

'You don't look very happy to be going out at this time,' Jack said. 'Have you got a hot date?'

'Yes, I have,' she said dismally, and wondered what he would say if he knew who with.

An American tourist, who had momentarily forgotten that the British drive on the opposite side of the road, had stepped off the pavement in the rush-hour traffic and been knocked down.

At such a time of day it would have taken a long time to transport the victim to hospital by ambulance, so the helicopter emergency service had been called out.

In the crowded city centre it was difficult to find a place to land and the helicopter had to circle the area for a few minutes before a suitable spot could be found.

When Hannah eventually got to her patient she found an elderly woman lying at the side of the road, crying out in pain from what seemed to be a broken hip.

She'd been alone at the moment of impact but was now crying hysterically for her husband who was in their hotel room across the street, unaware of the accident.

A police constable had gone to locate him and a senior officer was talking to the car driver who, obviously in a state of shock, was insisting that she'd walked right into him.

Bystanders were agreeing with what he was saying and one of them said that the woman had been walking unsteadily before she'd stepped into the road.

Hannah was only half listening. The woman did smell of alcohol, but that wasn't for her to concern herself about. It was her injuries that were her prime concern and at the moment, apart from a possible fracture of the femur, there were deep abrasions to the legs and ankles.

But an examination in a London street amongst the rush-hour traffic wasn't the easiest place to ascertain the damage done, and the sooner the patient was airlifted to the nearest hospital the better.

The helicopter was two streets away and the police had to clear a path for them to get through with the stretcher, but eventually they were ready to take off and when Hannah checked her watch she saw that she might just about make it to the theatre in time if they got airborne now.

Jack was at the controls and she was ringing ahead with details of the victim's injuries when the policeman appeared with the distraught husband.

He was in a terrible state and when she saw him his wife cried tearfully, 'I'm all right, honey. It was the wine.'

Her reassurance fell on deaf ears. His lips had a bluish tinge and he was clutching at his chest as he slid down onto the pavement. The policeman tried to stop his fall, but he wasn't in time and now he was kneeling beside the man as Hannah flung herself out of the helicopter.

There was no heartbeat when she listened to his chest or pulse beating in his wrist or neck. 'It's cardiac arrest,' she said urgently, adding to the pilots, 'Take the lady and come straight back. We're going to have to resuscitate.

'I'll do mouth-to-mouth,' she told the paramedic, 'while you perform cardiac compression. If we don't get his heart started again quickly there'll be brain damage if he ever regains consciousness.'

At first there was no response and Hannah was beginning to think that what would have been a pleasant holiday for the two elderly Americans was going to end up in a nightmare.

But she didn't give up, and at last there was a heartbeat—faint, but definitely a heartbeat—and he was breathing again.

She looked up. Soon it would be dark. It was time for

the Eurocopter to be tucked up for the night and here they were in a serious situation.

But Jack and his copilot were back more quickly than she would have ever thought possible, and as she climbed aboard once more it was with the knowledge that she would be radioing ahead to say that once again a life was hanging in the balance. A life that but for their presence would have already been lost.

By the time they'd handed the patient over to the trauma team that were ready and waiting on the roof of the Royal London it was eight o'clock and the hour of her meeting with Kyle long gone.

If he'd rung the operations room they wouldn't be there as their function was no longer required during the hours of darkness, so he wasn't going to know that she was still on duty.

It was nine o'clock by the time she got home, and all thoughts of a night at the theatre dressed in her favourite black dress, which she'd laid out that morning with joy in her heart, had died.

Where was he? she wondered. Had he gone without her? Or stayed at home? The only thing to do was find out and so, as the lift came gliding down, she pressed the button that would take her to his floor.

There was no answer when she rang his doorbell and her heart sank. He'd gone without her, and who could blame him? She went slowly down the stairs and, instead of going to her own apartment, left the building.

Hungry and tired, the last thing she felt like was making a meal, and the small restaurant where she'd dined that night with Kyle was nearby.

He was seated at a table in the corner with his face in shadow, but she could tell the mood he was in by the hunch of his shoulders.

He got to his feet as she approached and there was no

anger in him at this last catastrophe. Dejected would be a better way to describe his manner.

Pulling out a chair for her to be seated he said tonelessly, 'So where were you at seven o'clock?'

'Where do you think?' she countered softly.

'I have no idea.'

'You should have.'

His eyes widened. 'You weren't still working!'

'I was.'

He groaned. 'I don't believe it. How come?'

'It was the last emergency of the day and it was my turn. I could have asked one of the others to do it, but they'd have wanted to know why and I didn't think you'd want our theatre date to be general knowledge.

'An American tourist had been knocked down by a car in the rush hour. If that had been all I would just about have been back in time, but her husband suffered cardiac arrest at the scene and I had to sort that out before I could go back to base. It was half past eight before I left the Royal London. I tried to catch you at your meeting but you'd already left and were in transit, and I presume that your mobile was switched off.'

He'd lightened up a little, but there was still the air of despondency about him and she thought that this was something new for the man in her life.

Kyle was strong and resilient, the type who would surmount difficulties when no one else could. Yet the ruining of the evening really seemed to have got to him.

'Have you eaten?' he asked.

'No. I'm starving, but I felt too fed up to start cooking. What about you?'

'I haven't eaten either, so at least we can dine together if nothing else.'

He wasn't going to tell Hannah that the food would have stuck in his throat before she'd arrived on the scene. She wasn't the only one who was fed up. It was putting it mildly as far as he was concerned.

There had been devastation inside him when there'd been no answer when he'd rung her doorbell. For one stupid moment he'd wondered if that whining brother-in-law of Hannah's had turned up and dragged her off somewhere. But he'd believed her when she'd said they were no longer in contact.

He'd wandered into this place for lack of something better to do, and surprisingly Hannah had had the same thought. But it didn't make up for the evening he'd planned. The show, followed by a meal in an upmarket restaurant, and then…

She looked too exhausted for any reverting to that part of the proceedings. Would the day ever dawn when it was right for them?

When they'd finished eating Kyle said, 'Come on. I'm taking you home to bed. You're exhausted.' Her eyes widened. 'There's no need to look like that. I'm going to tuck you up and leave you…and, Hannah, take the morning off tomorrow.'

Kyle did as he'd promised. He took her home, waited until she'd undressed and was in bed and then took her a glass of milk and biscuits.

She smiled up at him from the pillow. 'I could get used to this.'

'What? Having me on the premises at bedtime, or being waited on?'

'Both,' she said softly. As he turned to go she added, 'When one has been tucked up in bed one usually gets a goodnight kiss.'

'Does one? Even though one knows what it might lead to?'

'Yes, in spite of that.'

'Right, then.' Bending over her, he kissed her cheek.

She smiled up at him. 'That isn't going to send me into dreamland.'

'How about this, then?' he suggested, and with his mouth on hers Kyle kissed her until she was breathless.

'Neither is that!' she gasped. 'I've never felt more awake in my life.'

'Obviously the wrong prescription,' he said laughingly. 'If it will help, I can take you on to the next stage of the treatment, but I thought you were tired.'

'Was.'

As she slid her legs over the edge of the bed Kyle removed her nightdress, and then, with his eyes warming at the sight of her nakedness, he began to strip off his own clothes.

It was like a journey to the stars, Hannah thought dreamily with his mouth on hers and his lean flanks covering her.

But, incredibly, when she awoke he was gone, with just a note to remind her that she wasn't expected at work until midday.

Hannah fell back against the pillows. She'd wanted him to be there when she awoke. To find him gone made it almost seem as if he regretted it. That making love to her was a thing of the night. Not for the cold light of day.

But whatever was in his mind it didn't dim the wonder of what had happened between them. They might have missed out on the theatre but they'd put on a show of their own, she thought as she went to turn on the shower, and hopefully it wasn't going to be a one-act play.

When she reported for duty after lunch Hannah saw that Kyle had someone in his office.

'That's the guy who's going to follow you in the training scheme,' Graham told her. 'How much longer have you to do, Hannah?'

'Three weeks.'

'We're going to miss you.'

'I'm going to miss all of you, too,' she told him with her eyes on the one she was going to miss the most if something didn't break soon.

Last night had been fantastic, but had there been any commitment about it on Kyle's part? He'd certainly not given her the chance to ask him. To some men sex was merely a release, whereas to a woman it could be binding and beautiful. She prayed that on this one matter at least they might have the same feelings.

'When is your next interview?' Graham was asking.

'Next Tuesday in Newcastle-on-Tyne.'

'Does Kyle know?'

'Not yet. I only got confirmation this morning.'

'Do you think you'll take it if they offer it to you?'

'I'm not sure.'

She didn't tell him that there was one health authority she still had to hear from and it was the most important, even though the vacancy was only temporary initially.

Every time she thought about it there came a vision of a small fair-haired boy on a new bike, who needed more than a father who had to work long hours...and a good housekeeper.

'Did you sleep well, Dr Morgan?' Kyle asked in a low voice when they managed a moment alone.

'Yes. Marvellously,' Hannah told him, glowing at the memory, 'but one thing spoiled it.'

'Oh?'

'I wanted to wake up with you beside me. Why weren't you there?'

'I wouldn't have thought you'd need to ask. Our early start at the unit. To be here for half past seven I need to be up at six-thirty.'

'I woke up before that.'

He sighed. 'All right. I went back to my own place because I felt that I'd taken advantage of you. I don't like that kind of thing to be a rushed affair.'

'What do you mean—that kind of thing?'

He supposed he should explain that last night was to have been a special occasion, which would almost certainly have ended up as it had, but not because an opportunity had presented itself.

Rather for a deeper reason, connected with love and commitment, and it was regret for the loss of it that had sent him back to his own apartment.

'Thanks for making paradise look like a barren desert,' she said flatly.

The interview in Newcastle-on-Tyne went well, but Hannah's heart wasn't in it. For one thing a letter regarding a post in East Gloucestershire had arrived that morning and she'd been able to think of nothing else since.

She was insane to let her career depend on a dream, she'd kept telling herself as she'd travelled to Newcastle. A dream where she was part of a loving family, who needed her as much as she needed them.

After her last battle of words with Kyle which, when she thought about it, seemed to have been more on her side than his, they were back to the old routine of polite acquaintances, and she wondered when, if ever, they would get their relationship off the ground again.

He'd asked her one morning if she'd decided where she was going to move on to, but instead of being her usual truthful self Hannah had been evasive, omitting to tell him that she had one more option to consider.

It was the place and her reason for considering it that was making her loth to impart the information. And on the day that she boarded a train to Cheltenham, Kyle still had no idea what her plans were.

As she came away from the interview her mind was made up. If she was offered the post, she would take it.

*   *   *

It was during her last week with the unit that the offer came, and Hannah hadn't changed her mind. The temporary post of consultant in the accident and emergency department of a busy hospital in a Midlands town was hers for the taking.

Kyle hadn't asked any further questions about her plans and she'd made no effort to tell him, but she sensed that he was tuning in to everything she did.

As for the rest of the staff, there was much joking on the unit as they professed to be devastated at the thought of a mere male taking the place of the delightful blonde who had brightened up their days, with Jack's voice being the loudest.

If the man in charge didn't join in they thought nothing of it. Kyle was extremely busy and there were rumours that he might be moving on himself soon.

Hannah had heard them with dismay. Where was he moving to? Kyle hadn't been there five minutes, yet there wasn't anyone who didn't think that he was the best chief they'd ever had.

One thing was for sure, if she died of curiosity she wasn't going to ask him what his plans were. If he wanted her to know he would tell her. She supposed that she was being just as secretive about her own new posting, so they were as bad as each other.

It didn't stop her from giving in to dread, though. Suppose he was planning on going back to Australia and taking Ben with him?

On the evening of her last day with the team they all went out for a farewell meal, and amongst the laughter and light-hearted chatter Hannah was acutely aware that one person wasn't joining in.

Kyle was standing to one side, glass in hand, and Hannah wondered if he was feeling as miserable as she was. It

shouldn't be like this, she thought wretchedly. Keeping se-
crets from each other. Acting like strangers. Allowing one
misunderstanding after another to eat away at them.

He'd seen her watching him and he came across. 'So this
is it,' he said flatly. 'You're off. Into the unknown. It's not
me who's doing the disappearing act this time.'

'No. It isn't,' she agreed calmly. 'But our paths have
already crossed once after a long separation. Who knows?
It might happen again.'

'You're prophesying a reunion every eight years?' he
questioned drily.

'It's possible.'

He turned away. 'Yes. Well. Let's hope we live that long
then.'

At that moment they were interrupted by a cry for a last
drink before they all went their separate ways, and as
Hannah fixed a smile on her face she thought what a dismal
sound the word 'separate' had.

It meant solitary. Togetherness was what she craved, but
the dark eyes meeting hers over the top of a glass had no
promise of that in them.

Kyle was the first to leave and Hannah wondered if it
was to avoid sharing a taxi with her. With the pattern of
non-involvement that they'd wished on themselves, the fact
that they lived in the same apartment block meant nothing.
But on occasions such as this they would be expected to
travel home together.

There was no sign of him when she got back to her flat,
and why should there be? If he'd had anything to say to
her the chance had been there when he'd expressed his
displeasure at her departing without a forwarding address.

As far as Kyle was concerned, her reticence was probably just an irritation. He wouldn't lose any sleep at the
thought of her moving out of his orbit.

*   *   *

He couldn't believe that she was doing this, Kyle thought as he lay sleepless in his penthouse apartment.

It was clear that Hannah intended to make a clean break. He'd known it from the moment she'd started hedging when he'd asked her about the interviews and, that being so, there'd seemed no point in telling her how he felt. If Hannah cared for him surely she wouldn't be doing a disappearing act?

It was two weeks later. The new job was good. Accident and Emergency in any hospital was always challenging.

If Hannah sometimes found herself automatically listening for the clatter of an approaching helicopter, she told herself that, whatever she did or wherever she went, the memories of the time she'd spent with the helicopter emergency service would always be with her.

NHS accommodation had been available and she'd taken advantage of it. It was basic but bearable and she'd thought wryly that where Kyle was moving up the housing scale, she was going down.

CHAPTER ELEVEN

EARLY on a chilly autumn afternoon Hannah found Kyle's parents in the garden, gathering together the leaves that had begun their seasonal fall.

She'd chosen a time to visit the Templetons when Ben was at school, as she didn't want him to find out that she was in Cheltenham before his father did.

When his grandparents saw her standing at the gate she was greeted with exclamations of surprise and pleasure.

'Hannah!' Grace cried. 'Where have you come from? Is Kyle with you?'

She shook her head. 'No, I'm afraid not. We're not in touch any more. I've finished my six months with the helicopter medical service and am now employed on a short-term contract in Accident and Emergency here in Cheltenham.'

'Bless my soul!' Howard exclaimed. 'Who would have expected that?'

'Certainly not your son,' she said smilingly. 'He doesn't know I'm here.'

'Why ever not?'

'It's a long story.'

Grace was observing her gravely. 'So why don't you and I go and have a cup of tea while Howard finishes bagging the leaves?'

He laughed. 'I see. It's women's talk that you'll be having, is it?'

His wife laughed, too. 'How did you guess?'

'So, what's wrong between you and Kyle?' his mother asked once they'd settled themselves in the sitting room.

179

'He only brought you the once and we were disappointed. He's been talking of buying a house. I believe he's actually found what he wants, but for some reason he's dithering and we wondered if it was something to do with you.'

She went on, 'From the moment we met you I thought, this is it. Our son is going to settle down at last. He's going to make up for all that lost time with Hannah. Was I being too previous?'

'I'm afraid so,' Hannah told her ruefully. 'It isn't that easy. I love Kyle. I always have, and I know he has feelings for me, but nothing goes right for us in our relationship. It's as if what happened all that time ago has put a blight on it and I think he's given up on me.'

'That doesn't sound like him,' Grace said, 'but I would imagine that his feelings for you are in a separate compartment of his life and he's wary of bringing them out into the open. Once bitten, perhaps.'

'It was all a terrible mistake on both our parts, but I'm sure he knows now that there was nothing in it.'

As Grace eyed her sympathetically Hannah went on, 'Kyle thinks that because I wouldn't tell him where I'd taken up my consultancy, I've done a disappearing act, but it's not like that. It was the thought of Ben and yourselves being here, and that there was a chance I might see Kyle occasionally when he came to visit that brought me to Cheltenham.

'I didn't tell him what I was planning because I'm never sure what he's thinking, but now that I've settled in I'm ready to give him a surprise…with your help.'

'Tell me what to do,' Grace said.

Every time Kyle went up in the lift the thought of Hannah's apartment being empty made him feel sick. It was the same at work. The new guy was pleasant and capable and the rest of them their usual affable selves, but it wasn't the

ame without her. Why had she been so secretive during
those last weeks? he wondered. Even if she hadn't wanted
to commit herself to him she could at least have said where
he was going.

Maybe she was letting him see how *she'd* felt when he'd
walked out of her life. Whatever the reason, he ached for
the sight of her.

He'd been home once since she'd left but it had been a
hurried affair. He'd only been able to spend a couple of
hours with Ben as he'd had a list of appointments as long
as his arm, but the next time it was going to be different.
His son was all he had now that Hannah was gone.

He'd been living the life of the joyless for almost a
month when he boarded a train that would take him to
Cheltenham and a peaceful weekend.

As usual his father was waiting for him at the station,
with Ben dancing beside him, and his spirits lifted. At least
he knew where he was with his own folk.

But his father's smile was missing and his heart skipped
a beat. 'Your mother's gone to Casualty, son,' he said.

'Why? What's wrong?' Kyle asked quickly.

'I think it's her leg.'

Kyle rolled his eyes heavenwards. 'What do you mean,
Dad...you *think*!'

'Best go and see for yourself, eh?' his father said. 'Take
the car. Ben and I will stay here for a while and do a bit
of train-spotting.'

Kyle stared at him. His father usually went into a flap
when anything was wrong with his mother, but not today
for some reason.

'Er...yes...right, then,' he agreed. 'Any message?' But
his father was more interested in the train that was coming
along the other line and telling Ben to get his notebook and
pen ready.

Was his father losing it? he wondered as he drove to the

hospital. His mother was in Casualty, and all he could think about was train-spotting!

He was relieved to see that A and E was almost empty. The last thing he would want for his mother was a long wait if she'd hurt herself.

'I'm Dr Templeton, here to see my mother,' he told the clerk on the reception desk.

She pointed towards the corridor. 'First room on the right.'

As he opened the door Kyle could smell coffee, and the first things he saw as it swung inwards were the back of his mother's head, a plate of biscuits and two coffee cups.

That was in the first glance. It was what he saw in the second that made his jaw drop. There was a doctor in a white coat facing her, with hair of the palest gold and eyes blue as forget-me-nots in a face he'd thought he might never see again.

'Hannah!' he breathed. 'What are *you* doing here?'

'What I've been trained for,' she said softly.

'But in Cheltenham of all places!'

'I wanted to be near your family for a little while.'

'My family?'

'Yes…us!' his mother said as she closed the door quietly behind her.

'I see. Or do I?' he said blankly.

As he sank down onto the nearest chair Hannah got to her feet and came to stand beside him. 'I thought that if you didn't want me at least I could maybe be on the sidelines.'

'Sidelines!' he cried. 'I want you in the centre of my life. I always have!'

'You have a funny way of showing it, Kyle.'

He was observing her warily. 'And you have a very strange effect on me that makes me say the wrong things…do the wrong things…'

'Not all the time,' she teased. 'I can think of one time when what you did was exactly right.'

His eyes were warming, the shadows disappearing.

'I can't believe you pulled this trick on me. I thought that Dad was going peculiar when he said he'd rather stay at the station than come with me.'

'We were all in the plot except Ben.'

He was on his feet, his arms reaching out for her. 'Is it all right if I propose to you again?' he asked with exaggerated meekness. 'I think I've got the words right this time.'

She inclined her head graciously and fixed him with laughing eyes.

'Yes, you may, but, please, don't be too long as this room is for emergencies only.'

'And this isn't an emergency?'

'I suppose we could class it as one.'

'Here we go, then. Will you marry me, Hannah Morgan, because I love and adore you? Life is joyless without you…and Ben would be delighted to have you for a mother.'

'Yes, of course I'll marry you, Kyle,' she said softly. 'My life is meaningless without you.'

'I don't believe this is happening,' he said huskily.

'Neither do I,' Hannah whispered, 'but it is!'

As his arms tightened around her she said softly, 'Tell me something, Kyle.'

'What?' he breathed.

'Will we be able to live in the house at Wimbledon? Or have you changed your mind?'

'I had changed my mind because it would have been just a shell without you there with us, but it's still on the market and a quick call to the agent will soon change that.'

'Brilliant!' she cried with her cheek against his.

'Anything else you want to ask me?'

She was laughing.

'Yes, there is. If we should come across my brother-in-law, promise me that you'll let him tell you about his problems as he always has a desperate need to unburden himself.'

'If it means that he's latching on to me instead of you, by all means, but the situation isn't likely to arise, is it?'

'Hmm.'

'What do you mean?'

'He's out there, waiting to be seen by one of the doctors.'

'He can be the first to congratulate us, then,' he said laughingly, and as they left the small consulting room with arms entwined they both knew that for the first time in their lives the way ahead was clear.

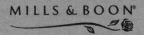

MILLS & BOON®

Medical Romance™

ACCIDENTAL RENDEZVOUS by *Caroline Anderson*

Audley Memorial Series

Audley A&E is an emotional place, but Sally is not prepared for the emotions Nick Baker stirs when he comes back into her life. He's been searching for her for seven years, and for all that time Nick's unknowingly been a father...

ADAM'S DAUGHTER by *Jennifer Taylor*

Part 1 of A Cheshire Practice

Nurse Elizabeth Campbell *had* to tell Dr Adam Knight that he was the father of her sister's child. He was furious that no one told him he had a daughter and was determined to be in her life – only that meant he was in Beth's life too. This fuelled their attraction, but were his feelings really for her, or for her sister?

THE DOCTOR'S ENGAGEMENT by *Sarah Morgan*

Holly Foster has been best friends with GP Mark Logan since childhood, so when he asked her to pretend to be his fiancée, how could she refuse? One searing kiss was all it took to make Holly realise that being Mark's fiancée was very different to being his friend!

On sale 7th September 2001

0801/03a

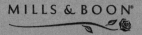

Medical Romance™

A NURSE TO TRUST *by Margaret O'Neill*

With a painful relationship behind him, Dr Dan Davis doesn't want to place his emotions in the hands of Clare Summers, his new practice nurse at the mobile surgery. He has learnt to trust her nursing skills; will he ever be able to trust her with his heart?

THE DEVOTED FATHER *by Jean Evans*

Kate Jameson is beginning to make GP Nick Forrester wonder if he has made a mistake by not allowing himself to love again since his little daughter's mother left. Maybe Kate's love is something they both need, if only he can find the courage to make them a family.

A SPANISH PRACTICE *by Anne Herries*

The warmth of the Mediterranean sun was causing Dr Jenny Talforth to blossom in front of Miguel's eyes, and he was finding it harder to resist his attraction to her. But resist he must, because he had commitments – and she was clearly escaping from something—or someone…

On sale 7th September 2001

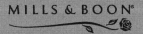